SLADE'S FALL

A BASTARDS AND BADGES NOVEL

ANDI RHODES

Copyright © 2020 by Andi Rhodes

All rights reserved.

No part of this book may be reproduced in any form or by any electronic or mechanical means, including information storage and retrieval systems, without written permission from the author, except for the use of brief quotations in a book review.

Cover Artwork – © 2020 L.J. Anderson of Mayhem Cover Creations

For Whitney - not only are you the best sister a girl could ask for, you're also an incredible woman with a heart and soul of gold. Remember, while life isn't always easy, it's always worth it. I've always got your back and I love you more than anything!

ALSO BY ANDI RHODES

Broken Rebel Brotherhood

Broken Souls

Broken Innocence

Broken Boundaries

Broken Rebel Brotherhood: Complete Series Box set

Broken Rebel Brotherhood: Next Generation

Broken Hearts

Broken Wings

Broken Mind

Bastards and Badges

Stark Revenge

Slade's Fall

Jett's Guard

Soulless Kings MC

Fender

Joker

Piston

Greaser

Riker

Trainwreck

Squirrel

Gibson

Satan's Legacy MC

Snow's Angel

Toga's Demons

Magic's Torment

"You can close your eyes to the things you don't want to see, but you can't close your heart to the things you don't want to feel."
~Johnny Depp

PROLOGUE

SLADE

"Motherfucker!"

The coffee mug sails through the air and shatters against the wall. Hot coffee splashes, hitting me on the back of the neck. I clench my hands into fists and count to ten, but the technique does little to cool the fury burning through my veins. Although it's better than following through on my fantasy to strangle Brandie.

"Brandie, you've got two seconds to calm the hell down," I manage to grit out.

"Or what?" she snarls. "You're gonna keep me locked up in this stupid cabin? Oh wait," she cocks her hip and taps her finger next to her full lips, "I'm already trapped here."

"Look, I don't like it any more than you do, but I'm not your enemy."

"Coulda fooled me."

Brandie spins on the balls of her feet and stomps toward her bedroom, slamming the door shut behind her. I heave a sigh as the windows rattle and hang my head.

When Brandie and I left our lives behind, I'd told myself

it was the right thing to do. That I was protecting her. And it's the truth. I *am* protecting her.

But who's protecting you?

The question mocks me. I don't need protection. Certainly not from a pint-sized female with a smart mouth. *And a hell of a throwing arm.* I shake my head at the thought. I've had more things thrown at me in the last two months than bullets have been fired at me throughout my entire FBI career.

Brandie is infuriating. And sexy as hell. My safety isn't the only reason I want out of this assignment, because that's what it became when I opened my big mouth and offered to protect her... an assignment. I want out because my cock can't take much more.

When she's not launching objects at me, Brandie is actually fun to be around. Her smart mouth is appealing in ways it shouldn't be, and her body calls out to me on such a primal level that I'm not sure what to make of it. I just know that it's too much for any one man to handle.

I know that this has been hard on her, not to mention the shit she went through before we rescued her, but I'm not her enemy. Of course, moving locations every week probably doesn't make me her friend either. But I could be, if she would just let me.

I make my way toward her room intent on explaining, *again*, why I've set the rules I have. I haven't shown her the text I received from Jackson earlier, but maybe I need to. When I reach her room, I register the music she's got playing, and wonder what she's playing it on. It's not like we're in a permanent residence where she has a stereo, and I took her cell phone from her back when we left.

I wrap my fingers around the doorknob and heave a sigh when I find it locked. Of course it's locked. Why I thought it wouldn't be is beyond me.

"Brandie, c'mon, open up," I shout through the wooden barrier.

I'd force my way in if this weren't a rental. As it stands, we have limited short term options for places to stay, unless we stay in a hotel. Every once in a while, hotels are fine, but sometimes it's just nice to have a place with a kitchen and multiple bathrooms. For someone on the run, she's certainly managed to stockpile a ton of girly shit. Make-up, hair products, lotions, and anything else you can think of are usually littered all over the bathroom counter within ten minutes of arriving at a new location.

I know we could stay in one of the safe houses, but I've been hesitant to do that. The people I'm protecting her from likely have connections far beyond what the FBI is aware of, and I don't want to take the chance of the safe houses being compromised. Maybe I need to consider it though, or at least take her opinion into account.

"Brandie, please, open the damn door."

I know she can hear me. Yes, there's music on, but it's not so loud that it drowns me out. I put my ear up to the door to listen for footsteps, and when I don't hear them, I start banging on the door, damages be damned.

"Jesus," she says on an exhaled breath as she yanks the door open. "What do you want?"

I had my words planned out, but they fly out of my mind when she's standing in front of me. She's wearing a T-shirt and panties, and while I've seen her in less, as in naked, there's something about the way she looks that barrels through me and hits me straight in the cock.

"Slade?" she asks when I remain silent.

"Hmm?"

"What the hell do you want?"

She cocks her hip and balances a slender hand at her

waist. I force my eyes to focus on her face, and it takes several tries before I can push words past my lips.

"Uh, we need to talk."

"Seriously? Because I'm pretty sure I've got nothing more to say to you right now."

"Shit," I mumble under my breath. "Look, can you please just put some fucking pants on and come out into the other room?"

She ignores my request for additional clothing and shoves past me. I roll my eyes and follow her, doing my best not to let my gaze fall to her ass and the sway of her hips. She bypasses all of the furniture and sits on the floor, cross-legged, which gives me a pretty spectacular view. I have to wonder if this is her intent or if she truly has no idea the effect she has on me.

"I know you think I'm controlling, but—"

She snorts and I glare at her.

"But, we're gonna need to find some common ground here." I pace the room as I speak. "I can't imagine what it was like for you when Luciano had you, but I'm not him and I want to keep you safe."

"You're right," she snaps. "You can't imagine. No one can."

Brandie had been given to Saul Luciano by Kevin Vick, both of whom had been the target of FBI and DEA investigations, as payment for a debt. Prior to that, Brandie was an escort, but regardless, she hadn't signed up for what she got. Drugged, probably raped, treated like a dog and held against her will. I helped with the bust that put Luciano in prison and ended with Kevin Vick's death. Unfortunately, Luciano has a daughter, Sapphire, and she's out for revenge.

There'd been another player in the game, Gary 'Stoner' Jones, but he's dead. My partner, Jackson, had been undercover and managed to fall in love with Brandie's best friend, Katelyn. After Luciano was sent to prison, his daughter and

Stoner purchased the strip club where Jackson and Katelyn met. Some shit went down and Katelyn shot and killed Stoner. While he's no longer a threat, his girlfriend is fucking pissed and out for blood.

When I read Jackson's text earlier, rage simmered just beneath my skin. Then Brandie asked if we could go do something, anything, to get out of the house. I'd panicked. Up until this point, we've been careful, but there's always been the added security in knowing exactly where Sapphire was because Jackson had been monitoring her movement. That all changed this morning.

I lower myself to the floor to sit next to Brandie. We stare at each other for a long moment before she breaks eye contact and pulls her knees up to her chest and wraps her arms around them.

"Is there more to this conversation, or did you just want to bring up the one thing I can't talk about?"

"Stop it," I snap. "Why are you always trying to pick a fight with me? I'm not the fucking enemy here."

Her gaze swings to me, and there's a sheen in her eyes that has my stomach plummeting. Brandie doesn't cry, much, but when she does, it's usually uncontrollable and makes me feel helpless.

"You keep telling me you're not the enemy." She squeezes her eyes shut, and a tear rolls down her cheek. She takes a deep breath but makes no move to wipe away the wetness. With her eyes still closed, she whispers, "Deep down, I know you're not. I believe you and appreciate everything you're doing for me, but…"

"But what?"

"It feels a lot like what they did." The words come out on an exhale.

Tears stream down her cheeks, unchecked and I can't stop myself from reaching toward her and wiping them away with my thumb. Her shoulders shake with sobs, and everything in me wants to wrap her up in my arms and promise her it'll be okay. But I can't do that. Not now. Not ever. This is a job, *she's* a job, and I need to remember that.

"I'm sorry that it brings back bad memories, but I promise you, I will never hurt you."

"Don't make promises you can't keep, Slade."

The way my name rolls off of her tongue is seductive, and my brain knows she's not meaning it to be, but my dick doesn't get the memo. I shift to stand up and turn away from her so she can't see what she does to me. I wish boners came with an on and off switch because there are definitely times when it's inappropriate, but unfortunately, it's not something I can control.

When I glance back at Brandie, my anger threatens to explode. She has so much passion, so much fire in her that seeing her like this, scared, uncertain, puts chinks in my heart that I thought I'd long ago repaired. No one should have to experience what she did, and the turmoil it's caused for her makes the words I need to say that much harder.

I take a deep breath and force the words out, knowing there's no way around it and vowing to get her through whatever comes her way.

"Brandie, Sapphire managed to slip her surveillance."

1

SLADE

A month later...

"I'm ready."

Brandie is standing at the front door with her arms hanging at her sides. Ever since learning that Sapphire is no longer under surveillance, her attitude has returned to that of a broken victim. She rarely comes out of her room, no matter where we're staying, and she hasn't thrown anything at me since that day. I never thought I'd say this, but I miss objects flying at my head.

"Let me just throw our things in the car and then we're outta here."

I step around her to exit the little cabin we've been renting. It's a vacation rental and we've only been here for two weeks, but I hate to leave. Not only does moving Brandie, yet again, weigh heavily on me, but the location is perfect.

Perfect for couples. You and Brandie aren't a couple.

As I toss everything into the trunk of the rental car—

everything's a fucking rental—I make sure to be vigilant of my surroundings. Sapphire is still out there somewhere, doing God knows what, and no matter how cautious we are, no matter that it's been months with no contact, we can never be too careful.

Satisfied that there are no monsters lurking in the woods surrounding the property, or at least none that I can see, I march back up the steps and cross the threshold. Brandie is standing in the same spot as before, seemingly not having moved an inch.

"If we hit the road now, we can be in the next state by nightfall," I say to her back.

She says nothing, just turns around and walks past me, her shoulder barely missing mine as she does. My eyes slide closed as I think about what it would feel like if she let herself brush up against me, if she didn't fight any sort of contact so hard.

I pull the door closed behind me and punch the code in that the rental company gave me so we could lock up. I jog toward the car and try to come up with where we're going to go next. This has been our routine for months, and it's definitely taken a toll on Brandie. There's gotta be something that will cheer her up or someplace that will make her happy.

By the time I join her in the car, she's already got her headphones shoved in her ears in an effort to discourage any conversation. I grip the steering wheel but force myself to relax when my knuckles turn white. After I turn the key, I make a point of cranking up the radio before shifting the car into gear and heading toward the car rental place in the next town over.

The drive is silent, other than the sound of our dueling music selections, and it remains that way for the first hour after we switch vehicles. When I pull into a rest area and cut the engine, Brandie pulls the earbuds from her ears and sits up straight, shoving her feet into her shoes.

"Hold up." I reach out and grab her arm to stop her when she opens her door to step out. Brandie glares at the spot where I'm touching her, and I pull my hand back as if burned. "You know the drill."

We've been to so many rest areas, and the routine is always the same. She waits in the car while I make sure there's nothing suspicious. Sure, maybe I'm going overboard, but I'm not taking any chances. We've avoided Sapphire this long and I'd hate for it to all be thrown to hell just because we have to pee.

Satisfied that there's nothing out of the ordinary, other than the man walking a poodle and talking to himself, I escort Brandie to the women's bathroom door and wait outside for her. She's quick and after my turn, we resume our drive. Brandie blocks me out with her headphones and tilts her seat back. It's not more than ten minutes before her breathing evens and she's asleep.

I open the center console and pull out one of the burner phones. Punching in the number I've memorized, I wait while the phone rings.

"Hello."

The voice doesn't belong to who I was expecting. I debate on hanging up because I know nothing good can come of me staying on the line, but I can't quite bring myself to do it.

"Hey, Katelyn," I say around a sigh.

"Oh my gosh, Slade! Is Brandie with you? How is she? Can I talk—"

"Whoa, slow down." I chuckle at the excitement in her voice. I wanted to talk to Jackson, get an update on Sapphire, but maybe it's a good thing that Katelyn answered. "Yes, Brandie is with me and she's, well, I dunno, not good."

"What do you mean?"

"She stopped throwing things at me." My tone makes me sound confused when really, I'm just pissed. The entire situation sucks.

"Well, damn. That isn't good. Is she eating, sleeping?"

"I don't know what to do for her, ya know? Any ideas?"

"Can I talk to her?"

"I don't think that's su—"

"Slade," Katelyn's sharp tone cuts me off. "Please? What harm can a few minute phone call do?"

I mull over the question, and while all of the bad scenarios play out in my head, there's one thing that surfaces and I can't let it go. Maybe, just maybe, talking to Katelyn will help Brandie. At the very least, maybe it'll make her smile for a few minutes.

"Fine. But five minutes and not a second longer. Got it?"

"Uh-huh."

I reach across the center console and gently shake Brandie to wake her. As her eyelids slowly lift, she pulls the headphones out of her ears and glares at me.

"What?" she asks and there's no mistaking the bitterness.

"Someone wants to talk to you," I say as I hand her the phone.

Since I'm driving, it's hard to watch Brandie and the road, but when the phone remains in my hand, I glance at her quickly. She's staring at the device, a frown on her face, as if trying to decipher who could possibly want to talk to her. Brandie tentatively takes the phone and brings it up to her ear.

"Who is this?" she asks suspiciously.

My heart squeezes at the uncertainty in her voice, at the fear. *Please, Katelyn, make her smile. Don't make me regret this.*

I can't hear Katelyn's side of the conversation, but I do hear Brandie's murmured responses, and the next thing I know, she's squealing and laughing. The shift in attitude is startling but welcome.

"Damnit, Katelyn, he's such an asshole."

I whip my head around at her words, my eyes narrowing on her smiling face.

"I know, right? He just doesn't get it."

I make a vow to tell Jackson to get his wife under control before she makes this assignment harder than it already is.

"Okay, time to hand the phone over," I say as I stretch my hand out, palm up.

Brandie huffs like a frustrated teenager and glares at me. When I don't budge, she says, "I gotta go. Love you, girl."

She slaps the phone in my palm and turns away from me to stare out the window. I put the device up to my ear, and I hear Jackson in the background, scolding Katelyn for answering his phone. He's not really mad at her, and she knows how to handle him, so I'm not worried.

"That was not a good idea, man," Jackson says when he gets on the line.

"Maybe not, but…" I shrug and realize he can't see me. I glance at Brandie out of the corner of my eye and shut my mouth. I'm not going to admit that it had been good to hear her laugh, see her smile. Especially when she's within hearing distance.

"Any news on Sapphire?" I ask instead.

There's no missing Brandie's sharp intake of breath at the name. Talking about it in front of her sucks, but there aren't many options at this point.

"Nothing. We've got taps on all known numbers we're aware of, as well as on her father. All of his communication is being monitored, and so far, she hasn't made contact. We've also got BOLO's across the nation for her last known vehicle. She's to be considered armed and dangerous."

"She *is* fucking armed and dangerous. I promise you that," I snap.

"You don't think I know that?"

I take a deep breath and try to calm my jangled nerves. I need for this to be over. I need to go home. Hell, I need to fuck away my stress and that can't happen as long as I'm stuck with a tempting woman who's the job.

"Listen," Jackson says. "Boss wants you back."

"What? Why?" I ask, even though it's exactly what I think I want.

"Nothing has happened, man. They say the man hours you're putting in are wasted out there. You have to be back by the end of the day tomorrow."

I think back to the last road sign we passed: 'Welcome to Oklahoma' it had said. I could definitely have us back in time.

"What about—"

"She can come with you, or she can go her own way," he says, knowing I wouldn't have finished my question with Brandie right next to me. "Either way, they aren't footing the bill for her protection anymore."

"Fuck!"

Brandie's head whips around and she stares at me. I can feel her eyes boring into the side of my head, and if she stares any harder there's going to be a hole.

"Yeah, it sucks, I know."

"This is a mistake and you know it," I argue.

"I do. But it's not our call to make."

"Yeah… Yeah, I know."

"So, am I going to see you tomorrow?" Jackson asks.

I glance at Brandie, and my stomach drops as I realize what her decision will be.

"Yes," I respond. "You'll see *me*."

2

BRANDIE

Two months later...

"What's going on? You seem, I don't know, off today."

I glance at the woman sitting on the overstuffed chair across the room from me. Dr. Timms is a therapist, my therapist, and I've been working with her for a month now. I wish I could say she came highly recommended, but the truth is, I don't know many people or have many friends to get recommendations from. I found her by doing a search in Google for trauma therapists. She was the third name that popped up, but the first two had been men and that wasn't going to happen.

"Yeah, I'm fine."

Dr. Timms smiles at me, and it's a kind smile. One that pulled me in from the moment I stepped foot in her office.

"Brandie, we've talked about this. Saying you're fine may work with most people, but it's not going to work with me."

She tilts her head, and there are questions dancing in her eyes. "Did something happen? When you were here last week you mentioned your fear that Sapphire would find you. Is that what this is about?"

This is why I always had an aversion to therapy. They can never let anything go, take you at your word. I probably would've kept going with that train of thought if I hadn't had a major meltdown one night in my hotel room. At the time, it had felt like everything that had happened since I took the job at The White Lily had come crashing down and threatened to suffocate me. I'd wanted to call Slade, and it was that thought that forced me to rethink and search for someone else to talk to. Someone who didn't know me. Someone who could be objective. Someone who I could give bits and pieces of the story to and they'd never know the difference.

I snort at the thought, and Dr. Timms's eyes narrow.

"What's so funny?"

"Nothing." I shake my head. "It's just... when I first came here, I thought I'd be able to only talk about what I wanted to talk about."

"Is that not what's happened?"

"Hardly."

"I'm sorry you feel that way," she says, and she sounds genuinely upset at the fact that that might be the case.

The hurt in her voice causes me to sit back and really think about my sessions with her, and when I do, it hits me. She's right. I haven't talked about anything that I didn't want to. She never forced me to open up about anything. It all just sort of came out.

"Damn," I mutter.

"What?" she asks.

"I guess I needed to talk more than I thought."

"Ah, yes. That's often the case."

I stare at Dr. Timms for a few moments, wondering what

her life has been like, about what led her to this moment in time where she is spending her energy helping others and not focusing on herself. Her life must have been very different from mine.

Jealousy snakes through me at the thought. I could have been her. Hell, I was on the path to being her. Sure, I always took risks and didn't always make the safest decisions, but I was driven, and I tried to never do anything completely stupid. Katelyn, my best friend, had helped with that. She was always the goodie-two-shoes in our group of friends, and she kept me grounded. Until I went to a strip club with a group of friends and got sucked into a life I never wanted.

"Let me ask you something, doc. Do you think it's possible for people like me to have a normal life? A happy life?"

"People like you?"

"Yeah, you know. People who are damaged. People who've been broken."

She stares at me for a long moment before she responds. "Do you still have that list that I had you make during your first session?"

I nod and lift my hips to pull the piece of paper out of my back pocket. I've kept it on me ever since that day. I unfold it and hand it out to her. She shakes her head, indicating she doesn't want it, and I lay it down on my lap.

"I want you to read me that list."

I glance down at the words I wrote and take a few deep breaths. I'm not exactly sure where she's going with this, but I'll play along.

"Okay. The first thing is 'get a job'. Then there's 'find an apartment', 'be safe', 'be happy', 'get a dog'." I chuckle at that last one.

"Is that all that's on the list?" Her eyebrows raise in question.

I shake my head. "No. There's also 'get married', 'have a family', and 'forget my past'." I glance at her with glassy eyes and realize too late that tears are spilling over my lashes.

Dr. Timms hands me a tissue but otherwise doesn't comment on my crying. "Do you remember what I told you after you wrote that list?"

"To take it one item at a time. And to not put a timeframe on any of it because everyone processes things at their own pace."

"Exactly. It hasn't been that long since everything happened. But guess what?"

"Huh?"

"You've already got two things crossed off your list."

I lean back on the sofa that Dr. Timms provides for her patients and blow out a breath. She's right. I buckled down and got a job pretty quickly. I waitress at a diner in town, and while it doesn't pay as well as what I was used to, the people are friendly and I'm starting to feel like I belong. My boss floated me a loan against my first few paychecks so I could rent an apartment.

"Healing is a slow process, Brandie. It'll happen but you have to be patient and do the work. The good news is, you're doing the work. Just have to work on that patience."

Her tone is light, and I realize that, for the first time in a long time, I don't feel like I'm being judged. She's pushing me, sure, and the work is hard, but she doesn't make me feel like less of a human because of my choices and where they led me.

The timer she keeps in the corner dings, indicating that the time is up for the session. It startles me, and Dr. Timms chuckles, as she does every time that happens. No matter how much I may resist, how impatient I may be, how *hard* it is, I always manage to get sucked into the sessions and forget about the time. I guess that means she's doing her job.

"See you in a few days?" she asks, as we both walk out of the office and into the waiting room.

"Yeah. I'll be here."

I pick up my reminder appointment card from the receptionist and shove my way through the door to the outside world. I tilt my head back and close my eyes, letting the sun warm my face. That was something I missed when I was held by Saul Luciano. The sun on my skin, the beauty of the world around me.

A car honks and pulls me back to reality. I head in the direction of the diner and try to push my thoughts away. One of the things on my list is to 'be happy', and today I'm choosing to be happy.

Screw the past.

3

SLADE

"Still nothing?"

I glare at Jackson, as I do every time he asks that damn question. He knows as well as I do that we don't have shit on Sapphire. He also knows that if I hear from Brandie, he'll be the first person I tell.

"Sorry I asked," he says with his hands held up as if to shield himself from the daggers coming from my eyes.

I return to the file on my desk. It's the call log from the prison where Luciano is housed. We've been monitoring his calls with the hope that something will lead us to his daughter. So far, nothing. There have been a few conversations with people who weren't on our radar that seemed suspicious, but those ended up just being the result of my active imagination and wanting to see things where they don't exist.

When I'm done sorting through the log, I shift my attention to my online search for Brandie. When she made the choice to leave, to be on her own without any protection, I'd been pissed. Not only was she making a stupid decision, especially with Sapphire still out there, but she also chose to leave me. The feeling is ridiculous because we weren't together, and she was only a job. Nothing more, nothing less.

Keep telling yourself that.

I have yet to track her down, but I've managed to narrow my search to the state of Washington. Brandie has no ties to the state that I'm able to find. No family, no friends, so I guess I can be thankful for that. If I can't find a connection, maybe Sapphire won't either.

Falling back on the one thought I can't quite let go of, I spin my chair around and face Jackson.

"You're sure Katelyn hasn't heard from her?" I ask.

"How many times are you going to ask me that?" he snaps. "Do you seriously think I wouldn't tell you if she had?"

He's not who I'm worried about keeping secrets. I know he'd tell me, but I'm not at all sure that Katelyn would tell *him*. I don't say that though.

"Jesus, I know you would." I heave a sigh and thread my fingers through my hair.

This girl has me so tied in knots that I'm doubting my partner. And that is something that can get a guy killed.

"Why don't we grab a drink after work?" he suggests. "And don't tell me you've got work to do. We work the same cases, and I know that's code for 'I've gotta keep searching.'"

The phone on my desk beeps, saving me from having to answer. When I hit the speaker button, our boss's voice comes through.

"Slade, my office, five minutes."

"Yes, sir."

I let go of the intercom button and glance at Jackson, my eyebrows raised. Not two seconds later, his phone beeps and he's summoned as well.

"Wonder what that's about." Jackson looks as confused as I feel.

I shrug even as my mind races with possibilities. Has

something happened? Maybe Sapphire has been located. Either way, I spend the next four minutes preparing myself for the worst.

~

"You can't be serious!"

Jackson wraps his fingers around my forearm to try and urge me back into my chair, but I shrug him off.

"Agent Cochran, sit down."

My boss, Supervisory Special Agent Michael Drake, is a nice guy, but he doesn't mess around. He trusts his subordinates but he's not above using his position and power to keep them in line. He's also the gatekeeper of the budget, and apparently, we're 'throwing away money' on trying to locate Sapphire and Brandie. Never mind the enormous amount of time.

"You know as well as I do that Brandie's in danger out there on her own," I plead, knowing it won't have an effect.

"I do, but you've gotta look at it from my perspective, Slade." Mr. Drake picks up a file and thrusts it toward me. "I've tried to find more funds for this, but they just don't exist. Not if we want to be able to work on any other cases for the rest of the year."

I look at the paperwork he handed me, and it might as well be written in ancient Greek. I'm not a numbers guy. I'm going to have to trust what he's telling me. I have to find an alternative. Mr. Drake goes on and on about the budget and other cases, but I tune him out. There has to be a way around this.

"Are you even listening to me?"

Jackson slaps my arm, and my head whips to glare at him. When he only tilts his head toward our boss, I wince internally.

"What were you saying, sir?" I ask after focusing my attention on him.

"I was giving you the details of your next case. Embezzlement by a federal employee…"

Again, I don't hear a word. I know he's talking because his lips continue to move, but it's muffled, like I'm under water. An image of Brandie the night we crashed Luciano's party appears, and after several seconds it morphs into an image of her when she chose to leave. She'd been scared, that had been clear, but what wasn't clear was if she was scared of what would happen without me there to protect her or of what would have happened if she stayed with me.

I stand up and flatten my palms on Drake's desk, leaning forward as I do. "I've got some vacation time saved up. I'd like to take it."

"Agent Cochran, we've been down this road. You only want to take your time to keep working on a case that I'm telling you has dried up." He holds his hand up to stop my protest. "I'm not closing the case, only shifting it down the list of priorities."

"If you don't want to approve my vacation time, then I'll turn in my badge and gun." His eyes widen and Jackson mutters something unintelligible. "What's it gonna be?"

This is by far the stupidest thing I've ever done. And I've got two ex-wives, a string of one-night stands and an unhealthy crush on a job on my list of bad decisions.

"You'd really turn in your badge for this? You feel that strongly?"

"Yes, sir," I say, without hesitation.

Drake steeples his fingers in front of him, and wrinkles appear on his forehead. He's trying to decide if he should take me seriously, if I'm an agent worth doing what it takes to keep on board. Knowing that I may have ended my career settles in my stomach like a lead weight, but I don't have the luxury of second-guessing myself now. It's too late.

"Fine," he says with a tight nod. "How much vacation time do you plan on taking?"

I plop down in my chair and exhale the breath I didn't realize I was holding.

"I've got about two months' worth saved up."

"Then that's what you've got. Two months to do whatever it is you feel you need to do. But when that time is up, you either come back and work the cases you're assigned, or I will accept your resignation."

"Yes, sir. Thank you."

I stand and reach my hand across the desk to shake his, but he ignores it.

"Don't thank me," he says with a bite to his tone. "I don't like ultimatums, Slade. Especially from someone who is supposed to follow orders, not issue them."

"Understood." I give a curt nod.

"Good. Now," he pauses and glances at Jackson. "Your new assignment is babysitting this yahoo." He tips his head toward me.

"With all due re—"

"You're really not in a position to be questioning me," Drake says, cutting me off. "Agent Stark, keep him out of trouble."

"I'll do my best, sir," Jackson responds with a tinge of laughter in his tone. "Sir, what about the embezzlement case?"

Drake waves his hand like it's no big deal. "I'll find someone else. It's an open and shut case, so it shouldn't be too difficult."

"Sir, I can't thank—"

"Two months, Cochran. That's it." He looks down at some files on his desk, which is his way of dismissing us.

Jackson and I exit his office and return to our own shared space. I waste no time loading everything I have about Sapphire, Luciano and Brandie into a box. Jackson stands there and watches me, his arms over his chest.

"What?" I finally stop and stare at him. "Spit it out."

"I'm just thinking of all the warnings you gave me about Katelyn. All the times you said that I needed to remember that she was a job."

"And?"

Jackson arches a brow at me. "And now here you are, about to throw your life away for a woman you barely know. A woman who was *a job*."

"Look, if you disagree with my assessment that Brandie isn't safe and that Sapphire is just biding her time before she strikes, then fine, don't help. But if there's even the tiniest part of you that thinks I might be right, is that something you're willing to ignore?"

Jackson's eyes narrow, and he appears to be thinking about the question, although I know him well enough to know he doesn't have to think about shit. Especially when it comes to the woman who caused his fiancé so much pain. And with four words, he proves me right.

"Where do we start?"

4

BRANDIE

"Hey, B, table four's order is up."

I shove my little notepad in the pocket of my apron and turn to grab the two plates piled high with pancakes and sausage. The breakfast rush is in full swing and the diner is packed, with a few patrons waiting on a table. This is why I love this job. Chubby's Grub has the best food in town, and the locals can't get enough, which means I stay busy and make decent money in tips.

"Here ya go, guys," I say as I set the plates on the table.

"Thanks, Brandie." Allen reaches out and touches my arm. "You're the best."

Alex, his twin, rolls his eyes, and I do my best to ignore the creepy skin-crawling sensation that washes over me. They're my age, at least I think, and Allen has been flirting with me since my first day as a waitress. I don't feed into his behavior, but that doesn't seem to matter. Everyone warned me that he's the town's resident playboy, and he's proved them right. I quit counting the number of girls he's brought in for breakfast, all with tousled hair and stars in their eyes.

"Let me know if I can get you anything else."

I leave them to eat their food and step behind the counter to check on the customers there. After ensuring that everyone is taken care of, I head through the swinging door to the kitchen and flop down in a chair. Chubby, the owner and my boss, chuckles at me.

"Tired already?"

"Yeah, but it's a good kinda tired."

I haven't told anyone about what brought me to this little town. I'd take tired over used any day.

"Well, Marilee should be here any minute. You can take a break then."

Chubby may come across as a little rough around the edges, but he's a giant teddy-bear. He's been feeding this town for thirty years and knows everyone that walks through the door. And the one person who walked through that he didn't know, he gave a job to. I can't help but have a soft spot for him.

"I'm here, I'm here." Marilee breezes through the door and tosses her purse on the floor next to my chair. "I'm sorry I'm late. Buddy threw up this morning, and I wanted to make sure he was okay before I left."

"No worries, Mar. We had it covered."

I return to the front of the diner and check on my customers again. Allen and Alex are standing at the cash register, money in hand. They seem to be arguing, but everyone is chatting so I can't make out their words. When I reach them, each has a guilty look on their face, but they quit talking.

"Are you all set?" I ask, focusing my attention on Alex.

"Yeah."

I go through the motions of ringing up their orders and taking their money. When the bell rings over the door to signal their departure, I exhale the breath I didn't know I was holding. Allen always makes me tense, but when Alex is with him, it's easier to dismiss. Or so I thought.

"Brandie!"

I whirl around at my name being shouted and feel my cheeks heat when Marilee is standing there with the cordless phone in her hand. I shake my head to clear my wandering thoughts and make my way to her.

"Phone call," she says as she thrusts the phone at me.

I stare at it for a moment, as if expecting it to explode if I take it. Who the hell is calling me? No one from my life before knows I'm here, and I don't have any friends outside of these four walls. Marilee shakes the phone in front of my face, forcing me to snap out of my stupor.

"Who is it?"

Rather than answer, she sets the phone on the counter and steps around me to handle the customers that just walked through the door.

I reach out and almost yank my hand back. When I grip the phone, I realize I'm shaking. Marilee looks at me with a funny look on her face, as if she's trying to figure out what my problem is. I slowly put the phone up to my ear and listen for a second before speaking.

"Hello?"

Silence is my only answer.

"Hello?" Again, nothing. "Who the hell is this?"

When the silence ensues, my heart starts to race and my palms sweat, making my grip on the phone slip. My eyes dart around the diner, seeking out anything or anyone that looks suspicious. The majority of the customers are regulars, and those that aren't are eating their meals. No one is on their phone, no one is staring at me as if waiting for a reaction. There's nothing.

I set the phone back on its base and head to the bathroom. I lock the door behind me, lean against it and force several deep breaths in and out of my lungs to calm my nerves. It takes longer than I care to admit. A glance in the mirror reveals my fear so I turn the faucet on and cup my hands under the cold water. Splashing my face helps to shock me back into some semblance of normalcy.

I manage to convince myself that there's no evil lurking in the shadows and my nerves subside enough that I feel confident in leaving the safety of the bathroom. I stop by each table in my section to check on the customers, forcing a smile and polite conversation.

My hands are stuffed into my pockets, my tips gripped tightly in one fist while my fingers curl around the pepper spray in the other. I only live a block from the diner, but it might as well be a hundred miles for as long as the walk home seems to take tonight. I ended up working a double—more than that actually—because Chrissy called off.

Turns out, that's who the phone call had been from. Why Marilee didn't just tell me that it was Chrissy on the phone, I don't know, but it doesn't matter now. Chrissy was sick and needed me to stay to cover her shift. Of course, I said I would. That's more money in my pocket to put toward a vehicle.

I reach my building, and before stepping through the door to walk up the three flights of stairs to my apartment, I glance up and down the street, making sure no one is watching me. I've never felt like I was being followed, never had chills down my spine or anything like that, but that phone call rattled me. For a few seconds, I was transported back into the hellhole I was kept in after being given to Saul Luciano.

After depositing my key on the stand by the door, I walk

across the studio apartment and drop down onto the bed, heaving a sigh as I pull the blanket up and over me. I should probably change out of my clothes, but I don't have the energy.

I haven't had the energy for much of anything lately. Work and therapy, that's it. Oh, and feeling a ton of fear. Fear doesn't give a shit about how much energy you have. It creeps in no matter what and refuses to leave until it steals everything you have.

I roll over and punch the pillow, trying to get comfortable, but it's impossible. An image of Slade flashes through my mind, and shock settles in when it brings a smile with it. Why am I smiling? Slade is an asshole who kept me locked away just like Luciano. The only difference is he tried to cover it up with fake concern and used the excuse of protection.

Did he though?

The silent question pisses me off, and it also makes me uncomfortable. And because I'm not a complete bitch, I recognize that it makes me feel this way because it forces me to acknowledge the truth. Slade isn't a bad guy. He *was* trying to protect me. He is no doubt still trying, even from afar.

None of that changes the fact that he's a man, and I'm done with men. They've brought me nothing but pain, both emotional and physical. The wounds may heal, but they leave scars, and those scars may fade, but they'll never disappear.

No amount of therapy can do the impossible.

5

SLADE

"Well, well, well…"

My muscles coil with tension at the sound of Saul Luciano's voice. He's sitting in a metal chair and is cuffed to the table in front of him. I glance over my shoulder at the guard and tip my head toward the door to indicate for him to leave. When he closes the door behind him, I return my attention back to Luciano and glare.

"I have to say, I'm rather surprised to see you here. Out of sight, out of mind and all that."

"Where is she?" I ask, ignoring his attempt at humor.

"Where is who?"

I pull the empty chair away from the table and sit down. I lean forward and keep my stare pinned on him.

"You know who," I snap. "You're not that stupid."

Luciano leans as far back as his shackled wrists will allow. He's got a smug smile on his face, and it hits me that he's enjoying this. He's trying to get under my skin, and I'm letting him.

"Agent, I hate to be the bearer of bad news, but I have no

clue where she is." Luciano tilts his head. "Last I heard, she and her boyfriend bought The White Lily. Maybe you should try there."

"Stoner's dead and Sapphire is on the run." I don't for one second believe that this is news to him. "Quit playing games."

"You think I'm playing games? I'm offend—"

"Cut the bullshit," I growl as I shove to my feet.

"I assure you, it's no bullshit!" Luciano yells, his face red and his eyes narrowed to slits. He's pissed, but I don't give a damn. So am I. He takes a deep breath and lets it out slowly before continuing. "My daughter is a grown woman and doesn't feel the need to check in with daddy. You tell me I'm not stupid. Well, *agent*, neither is she."

I watch his face as he speaks, praying that he gives something away in his expression, anything to tell me he's lying. The problem is, there's nothing. As much as I hate the guy, I believe him. Years of experience tell me that.

There's always the chance that I'm wrong, and if I am and he's lying, I'll find out. It just won't be today. I slap my palms on the table as I shove to my feet. With one last look at him, I turn to leave. Just as I'm about to pound on the door for the guard on the other side to let me out, Luciano's voice stops me.

"And agent?"

I glance over my shoulder at him.

"I suggest you find my daughter. There's no telling what she's capable of." He quirks a brow at me, and his smile is smug. "She had a pretty good teacher."

My muscles tense with rage, but I otherwise don't react. That's what he wants. And I'll be damned if I give an asshole like him what he wants.

I pound on the door, and it's quickly opened by the guard. I'm escorted out of the prison, and when I reach my SUV, I yank open the door slide in the driver's seat. I grab my cell phone from the center console and hit the speed dial for Jackson.

∼

"I could've saved you time."

I glance at Jackson over my beer bottle. We'd agreed to meet at our usual seedy bar to go over my visit to the prison. Not that there was much to tell.

"It doesn't matter," I mutter. "I had to try and we both know it."

"Maybe." Jackson tips his bottle and gulps the beer he's holding. When he sets it back on the table, he scans the room and then returns his attention to me. "Man, we've got limited time to figure this shit out. What's the plan?"

"Jesus, you think I know? Find the fucking bitch and throw her ass in jail to rot." I shrug. "Other than that, no clue."

"And Brandie? What about her?"

Images of Brandie flash through my mind, and I suck in a breath. She's the reason I'm doing all of this. She's the reason I can't let this go. Why, you ask? No motherfucking clue. She's a thorn in my side, and I can't extract her no matter how hard I try.

You haven't exactly tried.

I shake my thoughts from my head. "If we find Sapphire, then nothing. Brandie will be safe."

"You're saying you'll be able to just move on? Forget she ever existed?"

Is that what I was saying? And if it is, am I actually capable of doing it?

Yes... I think.

"Look, do you think you can get any of your buddies to go through the digital world? I've tried and I'll keep trying, but it's not my specialty."

"I can ask. Not sure if they're available, but I'll ask."

"Thanks, man."

My cell phone pings, and I lift it from the table to see I've got a text message. I type in the passcode to open the messaging app and the words I see make my stomach drop.

Unknown: Wrong move agent. Leave my dad out of this.

I read the words again and then again. I know the text is from Sapphire, and it briefly crosses my mind that she's giving me another way to try and track her down. That thought is quickly eclipsed by two more important questions: How the hell did she get my number and how did she know I went to see her father?

"Goddammit!" I slam my fist on the table, causing the beer bottles to shake.

"Care to share?"

I slide my phone across the table and watch as Jackson picks it up. His eyes narrow for a second, and even in the dim light I can see his face turn red with anger. Before it registers what he's doing, he's holding his own phone to his ear.

"Hey, it's Jackson. I need a favor." He asks whoever it is to help trace the text and then he listens while the person on the other end talks, nodding his head every few seconds. "I appreciate it. Thanks."

When he disconnects the call, he hands my cell back to me and then scrubs his hands over his face.

"Why do I get the feeling that Sapphire is ten steps ahead of us?"

"Because she is," I say behind clenched teeth. "She has been since day one."

"Well, she clearly knows what you're doing. Maybe that means she has no idea where Brandie is either." Jackson's voice is a mixture of hope and frustration.

"Maybe."

"Have you tried to call her lately?"

I snort. "At least once a day. I get the same recording every time. 'The number you've dialed has either been changed or disconnected.'" I mimic the robotic message that's plagued me since the day Brandie left.

"Why the hell do you keep calling?"

I shrug. I know why, but I'm not about to admit it to him. I can't get her out of my damn head.

"Katelyn hasn't heard from her?" I ask, knowing the answer.

"No." Jackson shakes his head. "Not that I know of anyway. She knows that it's dangerous for them to be in touch, and with the baby coming, I'm pretty sure she doesn't want to rock the boat."

"God, man." I heave a sigh. "I'm sorry that I dragged you into this when you've got so much going on."

"Slade, it's the job. I know that. Katelyn knows that. Besides, Sapphire is a threat to all of us, so I want to help."

"Yeah, well…"

"Stop," Jackson snaps. "Look, you can either sit here and wallow or we can get out of this dump and try to figure shit out."

I stare at him for a long moment. Part of me, the part that's his friend, wants to tell him to go home, protect Katelyn, enjoy this time in his life. The other part of me, the obsessed part, is grateful that he's my partner.

"Let's hit the road."

I stand and grab my jacket from the bench. I toss some bills on the table to cover the tab and we head out to our vehicles.

"Your place or the office?" Jackson asks before getting into his car.

"My place. I've got everything we need there."

"Okay. See you in a few."

Jackson follows me to my house, which is situated on the outskirts of the city. When I turn down my street, I'm on high alert. I scan every car we pass to make sure they're the ones I recognize as my neighbors. I don't notice anything out of place, and when I pull in my driveway, I allow my muscles to relax.

I hit the button to open the garage door and pull in. Jackson parks behind me, and after he walks in the garage so we can enter the house through that door, I push the button on the wall to close the garage door.

"Can I get you something to drink?" I ask when we step into the kitchen.

"Beer if you got it."

I grab two out of the fridge and make a mental note to grab another six-pack when I'm at the store. Jackson follows me to my office, and I hesitate before opening the door. He's been in my house dozens of times. Hell, he's been in this *room* dozens of times, but not since the boss man approved my time off to investigate this shitstorm we've landed in.

I take a deep breath and open the door, stepping through as I do. I hear Jackson's muttered 'Jesus Christ' behind me, and I scan the room trying to see it from his point of view.

My office is set up like a war room. Dry erase boards line the walls, and those are covered in pictures, computer printouts, and messy handwriting. My desk is shoved into a corner with my laptop and several computer monitors set up. And in the center of the room is a table, covered in research. It's a mess, and I know that. But it's also all I've got.

I don't give a shit how crazy this looks. I'm going to do everything I can to find Sapphire and send her ass to jail. Just like I'm going to do everything to find Brandie and make sure she's safe.

6

BRANDIE

"Fuck, fuck, fuck."

I'm racing around my tiny apartment because I overslept. Of course, my morning has all gone downhill from there. I could have made up the time easily, but when I went to get a shower, there was no water. Then I tried to use my dry shampoo and the damn aerosol sprayer was clogged. I'm out of coffee and bagels so no breakfast either.

I snatch my keys off the table and rush out the door, forcing myself to stop and lock it even though my brain is screaming at me to hurry. I rush down the stairs and out the front door, turning toward the diner.

As if my morning hasn't already been shit, it's raining and I don't have an umbrella. I pull the hood of my light jacket up and keep my head down as I speed-walk to work. About half a block away, the hair on the back of my neck stands up and goosebumps break out over my flesh.

I glance sideways toward the road and see cars moving slowly, but they appear to be keeping up with traffic and just being cautious because of the weather. I quicken my steps and mentally chastise myself for worrying. No time for that today.

When I reach the diner and grab the door handle to step inside, a car honks behind me, causing me to practically jump out of my skin. I glance over my shoulder, and there's a small white SUV parked by the curb. The windows are tinted so I can't see who's driving, but fear coarses through my veins anyway.

I stare at the car, and it doesn't move. It's windshield wipers and the rain are the only sounds I hear until the sirens register. I whip around, trying to seek out their source, and I see a cop car rounding the corner at the end of the street. When I glance back at the SUV, it's gone. I blink several times and shake my head. Am I losing it? Was I seeing things?

When the cop car passes in front of me, I turn back toward the door and enter the building. Warm air washes over me, but it doesn't help the shivers running down my spine. I'm probably being paranoid, but I would swear whoever was in that SUV was staring at me.

I scan the diner and nothing looks out of place. All of the booths are full, and Chrissy is scrambling to keep up with the orders.

"I'm so sorry I'm late," I say as she passes me with a full tray.

"Girl, it's fine. Just go clean yourself up and get out here to give me a hand." She winks and returns her attention to delivering the food.

I scurry through the swinging door to the back and ignore the glare that my boss tosses my way. I throw my stuff in my locker, and just as I'm closing the door, my phone pings. I reach back in to grab it and see that it's a text. Knowing Chubby is watching me, waiting for me to haul ass out there to help Chrissy, I toss my cell on top of my purse without reading it and get to work.

It isn't long before I forget about the mysterious SUV and the unread text. We're swamped and I haven't had time to pee much less dwell on anything outside of work. When the lunch rush is over, I take a minute to run to the bathroom. I cringe when I see my reflection in the mirror, the evidence of my shit morning staring back at me.

I try and finger comb my locks, but it doesn't seem to help. Nothing but a shower could help me now. Resigned to spending the rest of my shift hoping I don't scare the customers away, I head to my locker to check my phone.

When I read the text that came through earlier, my heart threatens to leap out of my chest. And not in a good way.

Unknown: Lucky u

What the hell?

I stare at the words and try to decipher their meaning. No one has this number other than my landlord, my therapist's office and my coworkers. While that should make me feel better, the text is so ominous that it only makes me more frightened.

"You okay, B?" Chrissy's voice breaks through the fog in my brain, and I glance at her. "You look like you've seen a ghost."

"Oh, um, yeah. I'm fine."

I shove my phone back in my locker, promising myself that I'll deal with whatever the text means later.

"You don't look fine. You were late this morning, you look like death and now you're shaking like a damn leaf."

I raise my hands and hold them out in front of me. Chrissy is right. I'm shaking like crazy. I clench and unclench my fists, trying to force myself to calm down. It doesn't work as well as I'd like, but it helps a little.

"Ladies, break's over," Chubby says from behind us.

"Geez, Chubs, give us a minute." Chrissy pops her gum and Chubby chuckles.

"You're more trouble than you're worth, ya know that?"

"Aw, you love me and you know it," Chrissy teases.

I've suspected since my first day at the diner that these two are more than employer and employee, and this just deepens that suspicion. They both adamantly deny it, of course. My gaze goes back and forth between the two of them, and there's so much sexual tension that it feels as if I could suffocate from it.

Shaking my head, I walk away. My mind returns to that text, but I don't have time to stress about it long because the diner is quickly filling up again and the rest of my shift passes in a blur.

At four o'clock, I grab my stuff out of my locker and breathe a sigh of relief when there are no other texts. Chubby is at the flat top grill, flipping burgers, but he stops when I don't make any move to actually leave. Greg, another cook, doesn't seem to notice and keeps working on the orders in front of him.

"Ya need something, B?" he asks.

"I, uh..." I shuffle my feet, feeling stupid.

"Spit it out. I ain't got all day." There's no heat behind Chubby's words.

"I hate to ask, but do you think, um, one of you could walk me home?"

Greg's eyes shift to mine, and Chubby's narrow in question. They've offered to walk me home before, especially when I work the closing shift and it's dark out. I've always turned them down.

Chubby holds my stare for several moments, as if giving

me time to provide a reason I want an escort, but when I remain silent, he shakes his head.

"Greg, walk her home. I'll handle things for a bit."

Greg's eyes light up. He's a high school student who seems to have a crush on anything with tits. He's a great kid, a football player with a passion for cooking. I bite the inside of my cheek to keep my laughter from escaping.

"See ya tomorrow, B," Chubby calls out as Greg and I exit the kitchen.

I raise my hand and wave at him over my shoulder. When Greg holds the door open for me, my breath whooshes out when I see that there is no white SUV parked at the curb. I was beginning to think I imagined the whole thing, but then I remember the text. My instincts tell me the two are related. I just don't know how. Or why.

"This way." I point down the street in the direction of my apartment building.

"I know."

My gaze whips to Greg, and I realize he's blushing. Shit, I need to get a grip. He's a kid with a crush because I'm female. Nothing more.

Get a grip, Brandie.

We walk the few blocks in silence. My eyes keep darting around us, taking in our surroundings, and I notice that Greg is doing the same. When we reach my building, I grab the handle to pull open the door and pause to turn and face him.

"Thanks, Greg. I appreciate you walking with me."

Greg glances to his left and then his right before focusing his attention on me.

"I can walk you up," he offers.

"I'm good. Really." I smile so he doesn't take it personally. "You better get back before the dinner rush starts."

He hesitates a minute before shoving his hands in his pockets and rocking back on his heels. "Okay. If you're sure."

"I promise. It's all good."

"See you tomorrow then."

With that, he walks back toward the diner, and I rush inside and up the steps. When I reach my apartment, my stomach bottoms out and I almost collapse right there in the hall.

Pinned to my door with a butcher knife is a note. I reach out with shaky hands and yank it free. The word 'Gotcha' is scribbled in what appears to be blood red marker.

Maybe I should have let Greg walk me up after all.

7

SLADE

"Hello?"

I was having the best dream when my phone started incessantly ringing. Not only did it interrupt some great sex, but I've never liked being woken up.

"Is this Agent Cochran?"

"Who is this?"

"This is Detective Lee from Jefferson County in Washington state."

I bolt up from the bed, my senses suddenly on high alert. It's been two weeks since I visited the prison and received that text. Jackson's contact made progress on locating Sapphire. She appeared to be making her way across the country.

"What can I do for you, detective?"

"Well, I think it's more like what I can do for you," he chuckles. Detective Lee sounds older, with years of wisdom behind his gravelly voice. "A young lady came in a few nights ago, pretty shaken up. She had a note that she said had been on her door when she got home from work. Poor thing could barely form a coherent sentence. What we did get was that her name was Beth, and she left the note with us so we could fingerprint it."

"Beth?"

"That's what she said. Funny thing, when we ran the fingerprints on the note, there was only one set, and they came back to a Brandie Carlisle."

My heartbeat quickens at the sound of her name. Is this the break I've been waiting for?

"Anyway, I pulled up her information and the photo attached to the fingerprint file matched 'Beth'. I also came across your BOLO for Miss Carlisle. Hence, this call."

"There were no other fingerprints on the note?" I have so many questions, but that is the first that comes spilling out.

"No. I figure that's for one of two reasons. One, the person who left it wore gloves, or two, Brandie is a fraud."

"She's not a damn fraud!" I snap.

"Calm down, son." A rustling sound comes through the line, as if Detective Lee is shuffling through some papers. "You know I've got to look at every angle."

"Right," I say with a sigh.

"I'm hoping you can shed some light on a few things for me."

I bark out a laugh. "I'll try."

"Fair enough. Why would Miss Carlisle give a false name?"

Why indeed? Logically, I know why, and it even makes sense, but if she's involving the police, surely she knows being honest is in her best interest.

"How long do you have?" I ask instead of giving an answer.

"Long enough."

I spend the next ten minutes filling in Detective Lee on Brandie's history, the previous investigation, and the current situation. By the time I'm done, my anger is off the charts and my determination to make Sapphire pay is stronger than ever.

"Damn." He takes a deep breath. "I guess that makes my next question more important."

My muscles tense at his tone. "Where the hell is Miss Carlisle now?"

"What do you mean? She didn't leave an address?"

"She did, but I went to see her today in the hopes that she could answer a few of my questions, but she wasn't there. I ran her information again, with the correct name, and found out where she worked. Her boss said she'd called off the last two days and he hasn't seen or heard from her since the shift she worked just before bringing in the note on her door. I'm afraid she's MIA, agent."

"Sonofabitch!"

I scramble out of bed, throw on some shorts and make my way to my office.

"My sentiments exactly. Based on what you're telling me, I'd say she's either on the run or this Sapphire lady got to her. Neither option is good."

"Is there anything else you need from me?" I ask as I start turning on all of my computers.

"Ah, no, not right this minute. Listen, I can't close this case as it stands. Call me if you get anything or if you find her? We'll keep looking on our end, but I know you've got resources we don't."

"Yeah, sure thing." I pull the phone away from my ear, and just before I hit the end button, my professionalism kicks in and I bring it back to my ear. "Listen, thanks for calling, Detective Lee. I appreciate it. I'll be in touch."

After ending the call, I dial the only number I have for Brandie. They say the definition of insanity is doing the same thing over and over and expecting different results. I guess I'm going insane.

"The number you've dialed—"

I stab the screen with my finger, cutting off the monotone voice.

Yep. Insane.

I glance at the clock on my phone and am shocked to see it's not quite midnight. I must have been more tired than I thought if I'd been in bed that early. I decide it's not too late to call Jackson, and I hit the speed dial for him, pacing back and forth as it rings.

"This had better be good," he growls into the phone.

"It is. Depending on how you—"

A pounding on my door interrupts me. I rush back to my room and grab the Glock I keep under my pillow. Whoever is at my door is starting to piss me off. They're lucky I don't have neighbors.

"Slade, man, what's going on?"

Shit. I forgot Jackson was on the phone.

"Someone's at my fucking door."

When I reach the door, I'm so pissed at whoever the hell is about to beat it down that I don't even bother to look through the peephole before throwing it open.

"Slade… Slade!"

Again, I forgot Jackson is on the phone.

"I'll call you back," I say as I lower the phone and simultaneously hit the end button.

I stare at the red head in front of me. Her green eyes seem to stare right through me, and the dark circles under them are evident of just how tired she must be.

"Can I come in?" she asks in a small voice.

This is not the woman who was going to 'take care of herself' and 'didn't need a man to look after her'.

"Uh, yeah," I finally manage to push out.

I step to the side, and she brushes past me. I stand there for a few moments, trying to wrap my brain around the fact that Brandie is here, in my house. And while she looks exhausted and scared, she's still sexy as hell and has the power to tie my libido into knots.

I shut the door, flip the lock, and then shove my Glock into the waistband of my shorts. When I turn around, Brandie is standing in the middle of my living room and wringing her hands.

Brandie lifts her head, and her eyes lock on mine. Everything about her calls out to me on a primal level. I want to go to her, wrap my arms around her and promise her that everything will be okay.

But first things first.

"What the hell are you doing here?" The words come out harsher than I intend because even though my thoughts are leaning toward protect-this-woman, my heart is bruised from her walking away.

Can't walk away from something that didn't exist.

And this is exactly why I've sworn off relationships. I have a habit of falling fast and for the wrong women. Hence the two failed marriages.

"I shouldn't have come here."

Brandie tries to rush past me, with her head down, but I grab her bicep and spin her to face me. Her eyes widen in surprise, and she frowns. I pull my hand away quickly and take a step back.

"Don't go. Just…" I take a deep breath and thrust my fingers through my hair, disheveling it even more than it already is. "Don't go."

"I didn't know where else to go." Brandie pauses and her tongue smooths over her bottom lip. Her eyes don't meet mine. "I think she found me."

"Yeah, I know."

Her gaze snaps to me, and the shock on her face is evident in the way her lips part to form an 'O'.

"How, um… how do you know?"

I stare at her a moment before making a split decision that could possibly blow up in my face. Under normal circumstances it wouldn't, but I've never been with Brandie under normal circumstances.

"C'mon. Let's get you settled in and then we can talk."

I turn to walk away from her, toward the steps, and I hope she follows. When I reach the top step, I worry that she won't, but then I hear the bottom step creak like it always does and know she finally unglued herself from her spot.

I wait for her to catch up and then lead her to the guest room. My cock begs me to put her in my room with me, but thankfully, my brain prevails. I flip the light on and grab an extra blanket out of the closet to toss it on the bed. I remember Brandie always liking lots of blankets. She said it made her feel safer.

"Do you have any bags in the car?"

She shakes her head. "No. No car." When I narrow my eyes at her, she continues. "I took a cab from the car rental place. Besides, I didn't bring any bags with me."

"Be right back." While I try to process the fact that she was so scared she left without any of her things, I get a pair of sweats and a T-shirt out of my bedroom for her.

Brandie is sitting on the edge of the guest bed when I return, her fingers curled around the edge of the quilt, her knuckles white.

"Here, you can wear these." She takes the clothes from me and holds them to her chest. "We'll get you some clothes tomorrow."

"Thanks."

"Why don't you take a quick shower and then come downstairs and you can fill me in." She yawns, and I almost rethink my strategy. Unfortunately, I need information if I have any chance of protecting her like she apparently thinks

I can. "I know you're exhausted, and I promise to let you sleep in. I just need you to hang in there a little longer."

When she nods her head and shuffles her feet to the adjoining bathroom, I leave the room and head to the kitchen to whip up a quick snack. While the tomato soup is heating up, I call Jackson.

"What the hell is going on?" he demands when he answers.

I wince at his tone. I guess I should have at least told him it was Brandie at the door before hanging up earlier. I take a deep breath and blow it out slowly.

"Brandie's here."

"The hell?"

"Look, just before she got here, I got a call from a Detective Lee in Washington state. That's why I called earlier." The tomato soup starts to boil, and I curse under my breath before turning the heat down and stirring it to make sure it doesn't burn. "I promise I'll fill you in, but I need to talk to Brandie first. She's in the shower now, but she's exhausted and I'm not sure how much time I'll have to get answers before she falls asleep and then wakes up and changes her mind about involving me."

"Fine. You've got until ten in the morning, but I won't wait longer than that."

"Thanks, man."

"Hell, I didn't ask you to do anything much different when it came to Katelyn," he says through a chuckle. "Speaking of, is there anything I can tell her? You know I can't keep the fact that Brandie's back from her."

"I know." I hear the shower turn off upstairs and realize I still have to make the grilled cheese. "Not sure if it's the best idea, but how about I just bring Brandie over there in the morning? I don't want to make a habit of it, at least not until

Sapphire's caught, but something tells me they could both use a visit."

"Sounds good."

"Okay. See you around ten."

I end the call and get the sandwich going. I hear the telltale creak of the bottom step just as I get the soup into bowls and the sandwiches on paper plates. When I turn around to put everything on the island, Brandie's standing there.

Her wet, red hair is hanging down, brushing the skin where my T-shirt slips off her shoulder. Her sexy-as-fuck shoulder. My eyes dip to her pebbled nipples peeking out through the thin, gray fabric.

"I, uh, I made something to eat." I point to the food unnecessarily. "Figured you'd be hungry."

For the first time since I opened my door, she smiles. "Starved."

We both sit, and while she digs in, I have to force myself to sit back and wait before bombarding her with questions. Rather than torture us both by staring, I eat, and it isn't long before every last drop of soup and every crumb are gone.

I stand to clean off the table, but Brandie's words stop me in my tracks.

"What if she followed me here?"

8

BRANDIE

The thud from Slade dropping into his chair causes me to jump. I hadn't meant to blurt out my fear, but I couldn't stop the words. They barreled out of me at what seemed like warp speed, and there's no calling them back.

"I have a state-of-the-art security system," he says, although his tone betrays his confidence. "If she followed you, this is the safest place you can be."

I nod but shift my gaze to a spot on the wall just beyond his head. I remember the last time I was in his house. It was just after the FBI got me out of the hell I was in. I remember that, although I was scared, I felt safe. Or as safe as I could be given what I'd been through. I certainly haven't felt that safe since, not until he opened the door when I got here.

"Brandie, can you tell me what happened?"

I glance at him, and something he said tickles my brain. "You said you knew she'd found me." I can't quite bring myself to say her name.

He rubs a hand over the back of his neck. "Just before you got here, I got a phone call from Detective Lee."

"Who?"

"He's working the case in Washington."

"How long did you know I was there?"

"I didn't. Not until he called earlier tonight." Slade looks at me with confusion in his eyes. "I tried to find you, believe me. Even if it meant I protected you from a distance, I just wanted to know you were safe."

"Why?"

He shrugs. "It's my job."

"It *was* your job," I counter.

"Brandie, don't. I don't want to argue with you."

"Whatever."

Quit antagonizing him.

Slade leans back in his chair, crosses his arms over his chest—his very broad, naked chest—and chuckles.

"What's so funny?" I snap.

"You. I see your attitude hasn't changed any since I saw you last."

"You have no idea what you're ta—" I slam my mouth shut and huff out a breath. "Whatever."

Slade sighs and stands to clean off the table. I help because otherwise I'd sit here and stare at his ass as he walks away. For as much shit as I've been through, and as much as he infuriates me most of the time, there's no denying that he's hot as hell.

After the dishes are loaded into the dishwasher, Slade grabs two beers out of the fridge and hands me one. I take a long sip, letting the bitter brew slide down my throat, and follow him to the couch.

We sit there in silence for what feels like an eternity before Slade clears his throat. "I got a few details from Detective Lee, but I'd like to hear everything from you."

"He's your guy, I'm sure he told you all you need to know."

"My guy?" Slade shifts to face me, pulling a knee up onto the cushion. "I don't have a 'guy'. Officially, I'm on vacation."

"Then who's Detective Lee?"

Slade looks at me like I've lost my mind. Hell, maybe I have. I showed up here, after all. "He's the detective working on figuring out who left the note on your door." When I say nothing, he narrows his eyes but still looks as if he thinks I'm off my rocker. "You know, the note that you turned in to the police?"

"How do you know about the note?"

"What do you mean?" Slade throws his hands up in the air. "Haven't you been listening? The police are—"

"I didn't go to the police!" I shout as I jump up.

"Of course, you did." He's arguing, but I can see the doubt creep into his eyes.

"No, Slade." I prop my hands on my hips. "I didn't. I got that note and got the hell out of dodge as quickly as I could."

"But…" Slade stands and starts to pace. "Then who the fuck called me?"

"I don't know."

"Motherfucker!" he yells and punches the wall to the left of his fireplace.

I watch as he tries to come to terms with whatever the hell all this means. I may not know Slade well, but what I do know is that he's a protector. He likes to be in control. And right now, he's not able to do either.

He stops in front of me and grabs me by the arms. His grip isn't painful, but it is startling. "Brandie, I need you to tell me everything. Every detail you can remember. Don't leave anything out."

"There's not much to tell. I mean, something felt off that morning and then I came home to a note on my door." I step out of his grip and retrieve my purse. I don't remember dropping it at the front door, but apparently, I did. "Here."

I thrust the note toward him, and he snatches it out of my hand. It doesn't take him long to read it. It's only one damn word. He drops the paper to the coffee table and looks at me.

"Where were you before you got home?"

"Work." He quirks a brow. "Jesus. I work at a diner a few blocks from my apartment building. It's decent money, and it keeps me busy."

I hate the defensiveness in my voice, but that damn quirked brow set me on edge. For some reason, I don't want him to think of me only being able to work as an escort. There's more to me than that.

"You said that you felt like something was off that morning. What, specifically?"

"At the time, I felt silly. I thought I was losing my mind, but I could have sworn that a white SUV had been following me as I walked to work."

"You walk to work?!"

"Yes!" I shout back, squaring my shoulders. "I thought I was safe. Besides, I was saving my tips to get a car. There's no public transportation and walking was the only option."

He thrusts his fingers through his hair. "Right. Sorry."

My body seems to deflate at his apology. He seems sincere, and I suddenly feel bad for yelling at him. What the hell is that all about? I've never felt bad about yelling at someone. Ever.

"Anyway, The SUV parked at the curb in front of the diner. I couldn't see who was driving because the windows were tinted, but it just felt like…"

"Like what, Brandie?" he asks softly.

"Like whoever it was, was staring at me." I shudder as I remember how cold it felt with the rain coming down, how exposed and frozen in fear I felt. "Then they were gone. Almost as if they'd never been there."

Slade steps up to me and opens his arms. I hesitate but

only for a split second before I step into them. His body heat seems to pierce my flesh and seep into my bones. His heartbeat jumps when I lay my cheek on his chest, and I feel my own pulse leap in response.

When I've taken all I can from his embrace, I step back and look him in the eyes. "Anyway, I was afraid to walk home after work, so Greg walked with me."

"Who the hell is Greg?"

If I'm not mistaken, there's a tinge of jealousy in his tone. I can't help but smile a bit at the thought.

"He's a cook at the diner. Nice kid."

He seems to release a breath at that. "How did he react to the note?"

"He didn't see it. When we reached my building, I sent him back so he could help Chubby with the dinner rush."

"Chubby?" he grates out as he raises a brow.

"My boss."

"Was anything missing in your apartment when you got home? Anything seem out of place?"

"You mean other than a note stabbed to my door with a butcher knife?" Sarcasm drips from my words.

"Yeah, other than that," he says, completely unaffected.

I shrug. "I didn't go inside. I took off."

"How did you get here?"

"I, uh, called a friend." It comes out sounding like a question.

"A friend?" The doubt is clear in his tone.

I huff out a breath. "My therapist. I called my therapist."

"Oh."

"Anyway, she knows everything that happened… before, and she was the only person I felt like I could trust. So, I called her and she agreed to take me to the nearest airport and she bought the ticket for me. Said she keeps a fund for her domestic violence clients in case they need to run. I didn't want to take the money. I'm not a domestic violence victim, but she insisted."

"Sounds like a pretty great person."

"She is. I, um, she's helped with a lot."

"I'm glad you found someone to help you deal with everything."

"Me too. But what happens when I can't continue with her? I can't go back there. Not while—"

"We'll find Sapphire. And you'll get your life back."

"And if we don't?"

"We will." He rests his hands on my shoulders and bends at the knees to look into my eyes. "I promise."

9

SLADE

"Maybe we should give them a few minutes."

Jackson's voice barely registers as I stare at Brandie, who is smiling and laughing for what feels like the first time since we met. Granted, it's not like she's had much to be happy about, and I should see the positive in not seeing this earlier. Had I seen her like this, I'd already be well past being a goner.

"Katelyn looks great," I say in an effort to steer the conversation away from my thoughts.

Jackson barks out a laugh and scrubs his hands over his face. "Yeah, well, I think Brandie has more to do with that than anything. Don't get me wrong, we've both been happy and are excited for the baby, but something has been missing." He tips his head to indicate the women. "I think it was your girl."

"She's not my girl," I snap.

"Right." Jackson walks toward the kitchen, calling over his shoulder, "You coming?"

I glance at Brandie one last time before turning my back on the girls' reunion. When I enter the kitchen, Jackson thrusts a mug of steaming coffee at me, and I take it gratefully.

"Since I'm not going to get anything out of Brandie for a bit, why don't you fill me in on what you can?"

After taking a few sips of coffee, I proceed to tell Jackson everything Brandie told me. The longer I talk, the more tense my muscles become. A hundred 'what ifs' race through my mind, and with each one, my anger builds until it seems to have nowhere to go except *out*.

Pain spreads from my knuckles, through my hands and up my arms, as my fist connects with sheetrock. The hole in Jackson's kitchen wall is a stark contrast to the cheery yellow paint that Katelyn painted it when she first moved in.

"Feel better?"

I whirl around at the sound of Katelyn's voice. She's holding a hand in front of her mouth, but I can tell by the crinkle in her eyes that she's trying not to laugh. I look over her shoulder and see Brandie, eyes wide and face red, making it difficult to tell if her reaction is fear or fury.

"Little bit, actually," I mumble.

"You're fixing that damn hole before you leave," Jackson demands.

I give a terse nod, but my eyes never leave Brandie. "Fine."

"Um, I'm assuming Slade filled you in."

Brandie finally looks away from me and focuses her attention on Jackson, and I do the same.

"He did."

"So, what do we do now?"

Jackson's gaze darts back and forth between Brandie and me. "Why don't we all sit down and we can talk?" He nods toward the living room to indicate we should talk there.

Brandie turns on her heel and scurries to the couch where she sits down and stays as close to the arm as she can. Katelyn follows her and sits on the other side. Jackson sits down as well, but I pace back and forth, unable to sit or even stand still.

"Brandie, Slade says you found the note two days ago?"

"Yeah. When I came home from work it was on the door."

"And you didn't see anyone or anything that seemed out of place?"

Brandie shakes her head. "No, nothing since that morning."

"The SUV?" Jackson asks in an effort to confirm what I've already told him.

"Yeah."

"Have there been any other incidents besides the note and the SUV?"

Brandie leans back and appears to think back over the last few months. After a few minutes, just when it seems that she isn't going to answer, her head whips up and her eyes lock on mine.

"What?" I stalk toward the couch, halting just in front of her. "What did you remember?"

"It's probably nothing, but there were some…"

"Jesus, woman, spit it out!" I shout, bending down to be at eye level with her.

"Get out of my face!" she shouts back.

I flinch at the vehemence in her tone, take a deep breath and stand up to step back. Katelyn and Jackson are staring at us with shocked expressions. I resume my pacing and shove a hand through my hair as I take a few deep breaths to calm down.

"What did you remember?" I ask when I finally come to a halt in front of Brandie.

"Like I said, it's probably nothing, but I've gotten some text messages that I chalked up to the wrong number."

"What makes you think that they were the wrong number?" Jackson asks.

"I don't know." Brandie shrugs. "They weren't threatening or anything."

"What made you think of them?" I ask, suddenly confused about why she even brought the texts up if she truly thinks they're nothing.

"They just never seemed to stop." Brandie pauses and takes a deep breath. "Even when I would change my number."

"Well that explains a whole fucking lot."

I resume pacing, and I can feel Brandie's eyes following my movement, as if her gaze is singing my skin.

"Uh, I'm lost. What does it explain?" she asks.

Realizing that I now have to give her a reason for something I'm not even sure I want her to know, I stop next to the fireplace and rest my forearm on the mantle. When I remain silent, I hear light footsteps behind me and then a small hand touches my arm.

"Slade," Brandie begins, and I look down at her. "What did you mean?"

I take a deep breath and blow it out. "It means, now I know why I couldn't find you."

"You looked for me?" Brandie's eyes narrow and soften at the same time.

"Of course. It was my job to keep you safe."

"You looked for me because it's your job?"

If it weren't the most ludicrous thing in the world, I'd think she was hurt by that, by the idea that she's only a job to me. I search her eyes for something, anything that would give me insight to her tone, but there's nothing.

When I remain quiet, she drops her hand and returns to the couch. I turn around to face her and the others, and I cringe when she grabs the pillow and hugs it like it's a lifeline. I look to Jackson for help, but he says nothing.

"What do we do now?" Katelyn asks when no one else speaks.

"*We* don't do anything." Jackson steps toward the couch and grabs Katelyn's hand. "You're not a part of this, so you do nothing but—"

"How am I not a part of this? I killed Sapphire's boyfriend. She hates me too." Katelyn stands and is toe to toe with her fiancé.

"You're also pregnant, darlin'," Jackson pleads, his face softening. "Work, home, and the OB are the only places you need to be right now." He holds his hand up when she opens her mouth to protest. "You have to trust me on this. I can't lose you. I can't lose either of you."

Katelyn's shoulders deflate, and she flops back on the couch, crossing her arms over her chest and huffing out a breath.

"He's right, Kate," Brandie murmurs. "I got you into this mess in the first place. I would never forgive myself if something happened to you." She rolls her eyes as if realizing what she said. "If something *more* happened to you."

"None of this is your fault." Brandie's gaze whips to mine at my words. "What? It's not. You didn't know how awful they were. It's not like you would have encouraged Katelyn to take that job if you'd known what was going to happen."

"Yeah, but—"

"But nothing," Katelyn interrupts as she scoots closer to Katelyn on the couch and puts her arms around her shoulders. "Those people... they're pure evil. Nothing we could do or say would change that. Besides, if it wasn't us, it would be some other poor girls and they wouldn't be so lucky to have these two to save them." Katelyn tips her head toward Jackson and me.

Brandie says nothing, but again, her eyes lock with mine, like she's questioning whether or not I still want to save her, protect her. I do, and that's likely not a good thing. At least for my heart.

"Fine," she finally says. "What do we do now?"

"You're gonna stay with me while we hunt that bitch down." My tone is far grittier than I intend.

"I'm not staying with you!" Brandie shoots to her feet. "I'll find a motel or something, but I'm not staying in the same house as you."

"You came to me, remember? I can't keep you safe if you're in some fucking motel."

"Well, you better figure it out because I'm not. Staying. With. You." Brandie punctuates her statement by jabbing a finger at my chest.

"Quit being so stu—"

"Brandie's right." Jackson's voice is quiet but full of authority. When I pin him with my stare, he holds up his hands. "Hear me out. She's got a life in Washington. Slade, you're on vacation. Why don't you go there, with Brandie?"

"Why the hell would we do that? Sapphire found her there."

"Think about it, Slade," Jackson pleads. "We're never going to catch the bitch if we have both Katelyn and Brandie hidden away. Maybe we'd get lucky and she'd move on, but to what end? So, she can do this to someone else?"

"So, you want to use her as bait?" I demand.

Jackson flinches at the accusation. As much as I hate to admit it, I'm not mad at him. He's doing his job. Much like I seem to *not* be able to do. If she were just a job, I'd have no problem with this. Shit, I suggested something pretty damn similar with Katelyn. The difference is, I understand why he had an issue with that. He loved her then, even if he hadn't admitted it to anyone, much less himself. That leaves one question: Why the fuck do I have a problem with this?

"Slade, I know you don't like this idea, but I'm supposed

to keep an eye on you, make sure you don't fuck this up." He glances back toward Katelyn. "I also have Katelyn and the baby to think of. If you go to Washington with Brandie, then hopefully Sapphire will follow, which means she's not here. You'll be there, so it's not like she'll get close to Brandie."

My anger flees in an instant. How could I be so stupid? Of course Jackson would suggest Brandie return to Washington. He's already lost one wife and son, and I can't imagine what he's feeling knowing that there's someone out there that could take another family away from him.

"We'll leave tomorrow," I say.

"What?!" Brandie's tone betrays her fear. "I came here to get away. I won't go back."

"Yes, you will. I'll be with you though, so you'll be safe." I sit on the couch next to her. "Jackson, Katelyn, can you give us a minute?"

"Sure," Jackson responds, and I feel the cushions shift when Katelyn stands.

When I'm sure they're out of earshot, I lift Brandie's hand into mine and pretend that it doesn't sting when she tries to pull it away. I tighten my grip and don't let her. I spend the next few minutes explaining what happened to Jackson's family and why it's important for us to go to Washington.

A tear rolls down Brandie's cheek, and when I'm done speaking, I swipe it away with the pad of my thumb. She leans into my touch, and for a moment, I forget that I can't have feelings for her.

Brandie takes a deep breath and says, "I guess we're leaving tomorrow."

10

BRANDIE

"Rest area in two miles. You need to stop?"

I glance at Slade and shake my head. My stomach is churning, but it's not because I have to go to the bathroom. Riding shotgun in a car with Slade is one of the better memories I have from this last year. He scares the hell out of me and simultaneously makes me feel the safest I've ever felt in my entire life.

And you pushed him away.

"Can you grab me a water?"

I twist to reach into the back seat where he put the cooler and smile when I remember our argument at the gas station where we stocked up on drinks and snacks. He was only going to get water, and I hate water. He also thought it was better to load up on healthy snacks. I pitched a fit because seriously? What kind of road trips has he taken? Junk food is a road trip staple.

When I hand him the bottle, he twists the cap off and tosses it behind him. I can't help but stare as his throat bobs with each swallow. He empties the entire bottle and throws that to join the cap. He turns the radio on and, despite the music, silence engulfs me.

I fluff the pillow that Slade brought for me and lean into it, trying to get comfortable enough to sleep. The problem with that is that the pillow smells like him. A mixture of Irish Spring soap, Tide laundry detergent, and his cologne fills my nostrils, and my eyes slide closed. The music fades away, and before I know it, so does the rest of the world.

"On your fucking knees."

The sting of the whip against my back is all it takes for me to collapse, giving Sapphire what she wants. The concrete floor is cold and unforgiving, but I can't let myself think about that right now. I need to focus and figure a way out of this mess.

"Why are you doing this?" I plead, hating the weakness in my voice.

"Because." She steps around to stand in front of me, but I don't look up from my position on the floor. "Daddy wants you broken. So I'm going to break you."

"You will never break me."

Sapphire shoves her fingers in my hair and pulls, the sting causing my eyes to water.

"Never say never," she says in a singsong voice, making my circumstances seem creepier.

"Brandie!"

I come awake with a start, sitting up so fast I'm surprised I don't get whiplash. My vision is blurry, and it finally registers that it's because my eyes are filled with tears.

"Hey, hey. It's okay. It was just a dream."

I swivel to take in my surroundings. Slade is sitting in the driver's seat of the car, but it appears he's pulled off the road. Semi-trucks rush by us, causing the car to sway, and somehow, the movement is calming.

"Where are we?" I ask when I'm confident that I can get the words out.

"Almost to the Iowa border. You about ready to stop for the night?"

"Uh, yeah. Sounds good."

I tuck my hair behind my ear and realize I'm sweaty. I'm always sweaty after a nightmare. Stopping for the night will give me a chance to take a shower and wash the remnants of my past away.

Slade pulls back onto the interstate, and it doesn't take long to reach the next exit and a place to stop for the night. I expected him to go to a cheap motel where we could pay with cash, so when he enters the parking lot of a Hampton Inn, I'm a little surprised.

"Is this a good idea?" I ask when he parks the car.

"It'll be fine." He opens his door, but before he closes it, he leans in and pins me with his stare. "Stay here. There's a gun in the glove box. I'll be right back."

Rather than wait for me to respond, he slams the door and I watch as he stalks across the lot with his hands in his pockets and his shoulders hunched against the wind. When he disappears behind the sliding lobby doors, I release a breath I didn't know I'd been holding.

"Damn," I mutter under my breath.

After what seems like forever, but is really only five minutes based on the clock, I push the button to open the glove compartment and grab the gun inside. I've never shot a gun before and I'm not completely sure I could if I had to, but I know I want to be sure I have the option.

I open the door and step out, closing it behind me. The only light is from the hotel and the lights illuminating the lot, but it might as well be pitch black out. My gaze darts around me as I walk to the sliding doors that Slade stepped through. I keep the gun in my hand but let my hoodie sleeve slide down to cover it.

"What the hell are you doing?"

Slade grips my arm and tugs me back out the door. Adrenaline must have been pumping pretty strongly through my system because I don't remember entering the building. Cold air hits my face and pulls me out of whatever trance I was in.

"Brandie." Slade shakes me by the shoulders. "I told you to stay in the car. Why didn't you li—"

My control snaps, and I yank out of his hold, my arms spread wide, the gun now visible.

"I was fucking scared, okay?!"

Slade takes a step back, his eyes darting back and forth between my face and the gun, as if he's been physically struck. His shoulders rise and fall as he breaths, and he thrusts his fingers through his hair. He does that when he's frustrated.

"I'm sorry, Brandie. I wasn't thinking." His tone is sincere, his voice low.

I drop my arms to my sides, but my stare never wavers. I search his eyes, as best as the minimal light allows, and guilt starts to creep in. I didn't mean to yell at him, but this is all too much.

First, I'm sold to a monster to pay off another monster's debt. Then I'm broken by a sick, sadistic bitch and her equally twisted boyfriend. Sure, I was rescued, but that hadn't ended their reign of terror. No, I've had to hide while also trying to rebuild myself and my life.

"Let's just go inside."

I heave a sigh and turn toward the car to get my things. Not that I have much. Slade stopped at Walmart on our way out of town, so I was able to get enough to get me through the trip, but that still only amounts to one small duffel bag with clothes and essential toiletries.

Slade takes the gun from my hand and puts it back in the

glove box, locking it afterward. We silently gather our things and head to our room. My legs feel like they're being weighed down by lead as I walk, and the closer we get to our door, the heavier they feel. Slade swipes the key in the slot, and after a quiet buzz, he pushes the handle down and swings the door open.

When I enter, my eyes zero in on the bed, the *one and only* bed, and I groan.

"It's all they had." Slade's voice is right behind me, so close that I think I feel his breath skate over my ear. "I'll sleep on the floor."

I toss my bag on the bed and ruffle through it to locate what I need to get a shower and change. Once I have everything, I make my way to the bathroom and flip on the light. Before I manage to get the door closed, Slade's voice stops me.

"I'm going to order room service. Do you want anything?"

My stomach growls loudly in response, and he chuckles. Heat infuses my cheeks, and

I'm glad I'm not facing him.

"Maybe a burger and fries," I respond and shut the door behind me.

I lean against the wooden barrier, careful not to bang my head and make too much noise. The bathroom is bright, with white tile and a white vanity. The towels are white, and even the complimentary toiletries are in mini white bottles.

I shake my head to clear my thoughts. I'm on the run with an FBI escort—a sexy-as-hell FBI escort—from a psychotic bitch who either wants me as her sex slave or dead, and I'm focusing on the stupid color of the bathroom. I'm losing my mind.

I turn the knob and let the water run over my hand until it's the perfect temperature. Once the shower is on, I strip and step over the edge of the tub. The hot water pelts my body, and my muscles slowly start to relax. The stink of my earlier nightmare washes down the drain, and it's not long before I feel clean enough to get out and dry off.

Avoiding my reflection in the mirror, I yank off the tags from the sleep shorts and tug them up my legs. Next is the baby-doll tee. Then and only then do I let my gaze wander to the glass in front of me. My physical scars are hidden, but my emotional ones stare back at me from eyes that seem to have had the life zapped out of them.

The funny thing is, until a few days ago, I would have sworn I was getting that life back. I was starting to feel like my old self, my pre-sold-to-the-devil self. One SUV, one weird feeling, one note, and I'm back to square one of healing. And the only person I want to do that with is Slade.

What the actual fuck?

After several minutes and many deep breaths, I square my shoulders and leave the confines of the bathroom. I step out and come to a halt when I see Slade stretched out on the bed. He's wearing pajama bottoms, and I suppose I should be grateful for that, but all I can focus on is his bare chest.

The way his pecs move when he lifts his arm and points the remote at the TV is mesmerizing. My mouth dries up and my lungs seize. It's not like I haven't noticed his looks before. Hell, it's not even like I haven't dreamt of him like this, only with a lot less clothing.

A knock on the door startles a squeak out of me, and Slade is off the bed so fast his movement is a blur. His eyes travel the length of my body, and when they settle on my face, he looks weird.

"Food's here," he says after he clears his throat.

Slade strides past me and air rushes past my lips from the breath I didn't know I was holding. As he deals with room service, I make my way to the chair in front of the desk. The bed looks inviting as hell, but I don't quite trust myself so it's best to avoid it for now.

The food is set in front of me, and when my stomach growls in response to the delicious smells, I cringe. It doesn't stop me from digging into my plate though. Not much could when I'm this hungry.

"I forgot that about you," Slade murmurs as he picks up his own burger and starts to eat.

"What?"

"That you are not shy when it comes to eating."

I swipe my mouth with the back of my hand and swallow. "Sorry."

"No need to apologize. It's one of the things I love about you."

My head whips to look at him just in time to see him slam his mouth shut. He averts his gaze and stares at the wall.

"I, uh… you know what I meant," he stumbles.

Neither of us say another word as we finish eating. By the time I stuff my last fry in my mouth, I'm beyond exhausted and fighting a yawn. Slade cleans up our dinner mess and chucks everything in the trash.

After he's grabbed the extra blanket out of the closet and a pillow off the bed, Slade gets comfortable on the floor. I don't move.

"I know you're tired and we've gotta hit the road early in the morning. Why don't you try to get some sleep?"

I crawl into bed and flip through the channels until I find a station that's playing reruns of some stupid cartoon. Within a few minutes, Slade's breathing evens out. I roll over and stare at the wall, fairly certain I'm not going to sleep. I'm almost afraid to even try because I don't want to have another nightmare.

I couldn't care less if Slade hears it or if I wake him up. I've spent a lot of time under the same roof as him, and I know he's heard it all before.

What I do care about is how empty it'll leave me in the aftermath.

11

SLADE

"I don't know what to tell you."

I thought that talking to Jackson would help, but it seems he's as clueless as I am when it comes to dealing with a woman with nightmares. I spent most of the night wide-freaking-awake because Brandie is very vocal when she's dreaming. I knew to expect that. It's not like I didn't hear it numerous times when I was first protecting her, but somehow, it seems different. It tore me apart as I listened to her toss and turn and cry out in her sleep.

"Did you talk to her about it?" Jackson asks, pulling me from my thoughts.

"No." I scrub a hand over my face and glance toward the bathroom door. She'll be out of the shower any minute, and I don't want her catching me on the phone talking about her. "I don't know what the hell to say. I want…"

"You want what?"

"Nothing." I heave a sigh.

A muffled sound comes through the line, and the next thing I hear is not Jackson.

"Listen, Slade," Katelyn says. "She's going to have nightmares. Just be there for her through them. I don't know why you're fighting yourself so hard. She went through a trauma, same as me. That doesn't mean she doesn't want to be loved or cared for."

"She hates me!" I argue.

"I don't hate you."

My head whips up at the sound of Brandie's voice. She's standing in the bathroom doorway in jeans and a hoodie, her towel-dried hair tumbling over her shoulders.

"I'll call you guys later," I say into my cell and end the call. I stand from the bed and make my way to the ancient coffee maker to pour Brandie and myself a cup. "It's okay, you know?"

"What's okay?" Brandie asks as she takes the offered paper cup.

"If you hate me." I take a few sips and try not to react when the worst coffee I've ever had slides over my tongue. "I get it. I'd hate me too if I were you."

"Why?" She tilts her head and looks genuinely confused by my statement.

"Well, because I'm a man. Because I keep you cooped up when you don't want to be. Because I can be an ass." I shrug. "Take your pick."

"What am I supposed to say to that?" Brandie hangs her head, and her shoulders slump. When she looks back to me, her eyes are glassy with unshed tears. "You're right, you are all those things, and yes, you piss me off, but I don't hate you. I hate myself."

Unable to stand here and watch her crumble, I stride to her and pull her toward me. Her cheek rests against my chest, and when she makes contact, the dam opens.

Brandie's body shakes with sobs, and all I can think to do is rub circles over her back and whisper reassurances. As she cries, she mumbles incoherently. Her words are almost impossible to make out, but what I do hear sets my blood on fire.

Broken.

Drugged.

Whipped.

When Brandie calms, she sniffles and pushes away from me, keeping her head down. I reach out to tug her back toward me, and she stretches her arm out to stop me.

"I don't know what you want from me," she says.

"I don't either."

Brandie raises her head, and her eyes lock on mine. That look, the sadness and fear in her eyes make it crystal clear that she's not ready for what her body is asking for. Hell, neither am I.

I clear my throat, and the sound seems to echo in the now uncomfortable silence. "We should probably hit the road."

"Right."

Brandie stands still for a moment longer before turning on her heel and returning to the bathroom, shutting the door behind her. It isn't long before the toilet flushes, and that snaps me out of my trance.

"You're not going to shower?" she asks as she puts her stuff back in her bag.

"Yeah." I stride toward my own bag and lift it on my way to the bathroom.

As the lukewarm water sluices over my body, my mind wanders back to the first time I saw Brandie. She'd been naked and covered in lash marks. Her face had been void of any emotion, and her body language screamed 'broken and hollow'.

The second I laid eyes on her, something inside of me snapped. I remember having to force myself to move forward, finish the task at hand. I remember putting her in an ambulance and wanting nothing more than to go with her but forcing myself not to. I remember going through the motions the rest of the day, and when I received the phone call from the hospital that she was going to be okay, I remember feeling elated.

I remember not a damn thing from that day making sense. And that hasn't changed. I still have no clue how to make my thoughts fit, how to make my reaction to Brandie slide into place with the rest of the puzzle pieces.

The few months we spent together had been out of duty. I was doing my job. The problem is, at some point, it became something more. Maybe it happened when she started to fight me on every little thing, when I'd seen that there was more to her than her experience. Brandie's feisty, smart, headstrong and so goddamn beautiful she scrambles my brains.

And therein lies the crux of the matter. I've been down this road before... twice. Not with a woman with so much traumatic baggage, but I have a history of thinking I can fix someone, make them whole again. Both times it blew up in my face. Because I did help them, they did get better and then they didn't need me anymore.

I scrub my hands over my face, closing my eyes against the now frigid water. Reaching behind me, I turn it off and fling the curtain aside. After wrapping the too small towel around my waist, I swipe the condensation off of the mirror and stare at my reflection.

All I see is a man that's become so jaded by love, by women, that I'm not sure he would recognize the real thing if it came up and bit him on the ass. I also see a man who wants love, who wants someone to share his life with.

When I'm dressed, I resign myself to facing Brandie again. In the time it's taken me to shower and get dressed, nothing has changed. Why, then, is there a knot in the pit of my stomach?

Because everything *has changed.*

~

"I'm getting kinda hungry."

I glance at Brandie out of the corner of my eye. We've been on the road for a few hours, and I'm surprised to note that she isn't hugging the door like she usually does. When I stepped out of the bathroom, following my shower, the air felt lighter, the mood brighter. We still haven't said more than a few sentences to each other, but we aren't avoiding anything either.

We're simply two people riding in a vehicle in peaceful silence.

"There should be an exit soon," I reply.

I pull into a McDonald's at the next opportunity and order us both burgers and fries. We eat as we fly down the interstate, and after I take my last bite, I can't take the quiet any longer, and there's one question that's eating at me.

"Can I ask you something?"

Brandie's head whips in my direction, as if startled by my voice. "Ah, sure."

"Why do you hate yourself?" It makes no sense to me. She's young, pretty, smart, and did nothing wrong.

She laughs, but it's empty, humorless and then she turns to stare out the window. Several minutes pass, and I kick myself for asking. Clearly she doesn't want to talk about it and I'm not he—

"Because I'm weak." Her voice sounds small, frustrated, scared.

I can't stop the snort that escapes. "Sorry," I say when she glares at me. "But I don't get it. How in the hell can you possibly think you're weak?"

Her glare turns into an incredulous stare. Her lips part,

and her cheeks flush. She's twisting her hands in her lap, and it's several tense moments before she speaks.

"You don't know the things I did." Her voice is so quiet I almost miss the words. "I let her break me."

This is what some would call a pivotal moment, one that has two equally shitty paths to very different outcomes. I can veer left or right and avoid what I know is going to be a miserable conversation for her, *or* I can stay the course and encourage her to tell me everything that happened and be there to pick up the pieces when she feels victimized all over again. As uncomfortable either option makes me, this isn't about me. If we're going to be thrown together for the foreseeable future, I need to know what happened. I need to know what's not in the official reports.

"You know you can tell me anything, right?"

"You've read the reports. Hell, you took most of my statements."

"True, but by your own admission, I don't know everything."

"Can we just drop it? Please?"

"No." I shake my head. "No, Brandie, we can't drop it. I know I piss you off, and I know this isn't easy for you, but it's not something that you can just tuck away and forget."

"I'll never forget it," she shouts, and I have to fight the tilt of my lips into a grin at her fire. "Not for one second will that time ever not have happened. I will carry it with me and live with it for the rest of my life."

"True. But wouldn't it be better to let someone help you carry the load? You're not alone, ya know?"

"What? You wanna help?" Her brows lift in skepticism. "You don't even know me! Not really. Not beyond the fact that I'm—"

"Maybe I want to get to know you."

Her mouth slams shut, and her eyes narrow. "I don't understand."

"Me either," I mutter. "Brandie, I can't explain it."

"Maybe you should try," she suggests with a hint of demand in her tone.

I keep my focus on the road stretched out before us, but my thoughts are on the woman beside me. How do I explain to her, without sounding like a total creep, that I can't get her out of my head? That, despite all of the reasons I shouldn't, I like her? That for whatever reason, she means more to me than just a job?

"It's not that easy," I settle on. "I can't even explain it to myself." I take my eyes off the road for a moment and glance at her. She's chewing her bottom lip, and the action sends a jolt of electricity to my dick. I shake my head to clear my thoughts and return my eyes to the road.

"When you decided to leave, I told myself it was the right thing. I tried to convince myself that you were nothing to me other than a victim or a witness or whatever. I failed miserably."

"Why?" The word comes out on a sigh.

"I. Don't. Know." I shove shaky fingers through my hair while my free hand remains on the steering wheel. "You'd been through so much, yet there's this fire in you. You threw things at me, insulted me, drove me fucking insane, but I still wanted to be around you. I wanted to be the person to keep you safe, the man who made you *feel* safe."

"You did make me feel safe. You still do."

"Then why did you choose to leave?" It's not a question I have a right to ask, but my curiosity forces the words past my lips.

"I had to, Slade." She licks her lips. "I had to find *me* again. I still do. I need to learn to trust myself again."

I consider that, let the statement ruminate in my brain. It

makes sense, and she's right. She needs to be comfortable in her own skin before she can be comfortable with anyone else getting close. Is that what I want? To be close to her? To be more to her than just a protector?

Yes.

The answer hits me with the speed of a whizzing bullet. For whatever reason, Brandie is in my head, and she's taken up residence whether she means to or not. My history with women and relationships should have me running, but instead, I'm holding on for dear life.

I realize that I've remained silent for too long, and I can feel Brandie's gaze burning a hole in the side of my head. I take several deep breaths before leaping into what could be nothing more than a waiting pit of heartbreak.

"Let me help with that."

12

BRANDIE

Let me help with that.

When Slade uttered those words, my heart skipped a beat. Maybe it was the words themselves or maybe it was the sincerity I heard in them. Either way, I know that we need to have a long talk before I can even consider trusting him. I guess the more accurate statement is that I want to trust myself with him. I want to and that, more than anything, scares the hell out of me. I don't exactly have a great track record when it comes to making smart decisions.

The rest of the drive passes in a quiet blur. Slade makes the decision to stop for the night, and while it's hard being in such close proximity to him, I'm grateful. It gives me more time to get used to the idea of him seeing where I live, where I chose to make my home. Even more difficult is getting used to the idea that I'm letting him into my world. My personal space.

Slade guides me toward our room, never letting me trail behind him. My eyes dart back and forth as we walk in the dark. I understand why he chooses these dumpy motels, but I'd feel a lot better if we were walking in a lighted hallway versus outside where the lights are either flickering or busted.

"This is us," he says as he puts a hand on my bicep to stop me in front of the door.

He sticks the keycard in the slot and when the little green light flashes and when the mechanism beeps, he pulls it out and opens the door. I make no move to enter, knowing that he'll want to clear the room before I do.

After ensuring that there are no monsters lurking, he motions for me to join him inside. I shut the door and fasten the chain lock, along with flipping the deadbolt. When I turn around, Slade is right there, causing me to jump.

My hand goes to my throat, and I squeak, "Jesus, you scared me."

"Sorry." Slade brushes my cheek with his fingertips, and I lean into his touch. "You are so goddamn beautiful."

Slade's lips press against mine, and it's so feather-light, so gentle. The kiss ends before it can really begin, and I feel him pull away from me, feel the loss of his body heat. When a chill wracks my body, I open my eyes and see him standing a few feet away with his back to me and his feet braced apart.

"Wh-what was that for?"

His shoulders rise and fall as his head dips down. "I had to."

"Did you have to stop, too?"

I slam my mouth shut, and Slade whirls around with wide eyes. Heat creeps up my neck and blooms across my face. I can't believe I let those words fly out of my mouth.

Stupid. So stupid.

"I think it's my turn to ask this." Slade takes a step closer. "What do you want from me?"

"I…" I swallow past the lump in my throat. "I don't know."

"Well, that clears things up," he says, but punctuates it with a chuckle, and suddenly, the tension is gone.

"Slade, I just want to be normal again. I don't want my trauma to define me. I just… I want what everybody wants, I guess."

"Love, marriage, two point five kids, a dog and a white picket fence?" Sarcasm drips from his tone, but for some reason, it's not offensive.

A smile curves my lips, and I don't try to hide it. "Well, yeah." I shrug. "Sort of. I want all of that, eventually. Right now, from you, I just want whatever is real."

"What's real for you, Brandie?"

Slade's eyes bore into mine, and it takes all of my willpower now to look away.

"I don't hate you," I whisper.

Slade takes a step toward me. "That's a start." His smile grows. "And?"

I swallow as I try to find my words. "I feel safe with you."

That gorgeous grin widens. "And?" Another step closer.

"You make me nervous."

His smile falters, but only for a second. "How nervous?" he asks and takes yet another step closer.

He's within touching distance now, and while he doesn't reach out, it feels as if there's an invisible string pulling me toward him. I take a step in his direction, my knees shaking and my heart pounding.

"Very nervous," I finally say.

"I can work with that."

That statement is one that haunts me, but I force myself to remember that Slade wouldn't know that. When he lifts his foot to take that last step, I hold up my hand to stop him.

"Wait!" Slade arches one perfect brow and tilts his head in question. "You also scare me."

If words were a physical punch, the look on his face tells me I just landed a brutal blow. He takes a step backward, and my shoulders slump.

"I would never hurt you. You have to know that."

"I know. At least, I know you'd never physically hurt me." I wrap my arms around myself as if to protect myself from the emotion flowing from him. "But I'm not normal, Slade. I'm a victim. I have issues." I take a deep breath, blow it out slowly, and glance around the room at anything and everything that isn't male perfection. "I'd be useless in a relationship. I have demons that won't quit, and I'm scared. I like you, and I have no idea why or what to do about it. A year ago, I'd have jumped in with both feet and damned the consequences, but I'm not that girl anymore."

"But you do like me?" he asks, and there's a tiny bit of hope in his voice.

"I think so. But how do I know it's real and not just a reaction to the circumstances?"

"You don't. But neither do I."

"I'm not sure what to do with that… about that."

Slade invades my space, and when he picks up my hand and holds it in his, warmth floods my system. With his free hand, he grips the back of my neck and pulls me toward him, much like he had when I'd been crying earlier. He rests his cheek on the top of my head, and his breath tickles my scalp.

"We both have a lot of baggage." He presses more firmly against me when I try to raise my head. "Brandie, I have a past too. Granted, it pales in comparison to yours, but it still left scars. Massive ones as far as I'm concerned. But I know that I can't get you out of my head, and I want to know why. I want to see what this is." He sighs and kisses my hair. "If it's just the circumstances, then we go our separate ways when this is all over. But if it's not? If there really is something between us, don't you think we've both suffered enough? Don't you think we owe it to ourselves to at least see?"

What he says makes sense, especially when he puts it like that. And I do want something good right now. But I can't shake the fear. I'm no longer able to set aside the 'what if's' like I used to. But I want to. God, I want to.

With a determination that is still shaky at best, I nod against his chest.

I'm willing to try if he is.

∼

Slade's even breathing is the only sound in the room, and I wish it were enough to lull me to sleep. We're in separate beds because even though we agreed to give this, whatever the fuck *this* is, a try, I wasn't ready to invite him into my bed.

I toss and turn and go back over our conversation in my mind. He said he has baggage too, and I wonder what that is. At the time, I'd been so wrapped up in everything else he'd said that I hadn't thought to ask. Maybe I should have.

Giving up on trying to sleep, I grab the remote off of the nightstand between the two beds and switch on the television. I flip through the channels until I come to reruns of *I love Lucy* and after watching two episodes, I feel my eyelids grow heavy. I roll to my side and pull the covers up to my chin and finally drift into sleep.

"Never say never." Sapphire's tone sends shivers down my spine and they seem to disappear into the concrete under my knees. "You're all the same. You think you're strong, that you can stand up to Daddy and survive me. But just like the others, I've got some surprises in store."

"You ready for me, babe?"

I recognize that voice but can't quite place it. Black boots enter my line of vision, and I try to raise my head to see who they belong to, but Sapphire's grip is too tight and I can't.

"Just about," Sapphire responds to the unknown addition to the room.

The biting pain of the whip brings tears to my eyes, but I refuse to let them fall. With each strike, my hold on consciousness slips, and by the fifth strike, black dots dance in front of me. On the sixth strike, I give in and slump to the floor.

I toss and turn, the dingy motel sheets wrapping around my torso as I do.

Animalistic grunts reach through the haze and pull me out of the darkness. I wince when I try to sit up and feel the cracking of dried blood across my back. When I finally get to my knees and I adjust to the dim lighting, a pair of eyes stare at me over Sapphire's shoulder.

When he registers that I'm staring right back, an evil grin spreads across his face. I lower my gaze, and that's when I realize that the grunts I heard are Sapphire's and his. Sapphire's legs are wrapped around the man's body and her naked ass is on full display. His pants are around his ankles and rest on the black boots from earlier. They're going at it like rabbits.

"We have an audience," the man says.

Sapphire looks over her shoulder at me and grins. When I don't react, her grin falters and she narrows her eyes. "Show some fucking respect!" An eerie sereneness washes over her. "Say 'hello' to my boyfriend, Stoner."

Are these two for real? Surely she doesn't expect me to act like I'm greeting dinner guests for a housewarming party. Again, when I don't react or make any move to do as she says, her facade starts to crumble. Mid thrust, she lowers her legs and pats Stoner's chest like she would a dog.

She walks toward me, the heels of her stilettos clicking on the floor. She's naked except for those shoes, and I force myself to focus on them. When her feet are inches from my knees, she stops... and nothing happens. No whip, no taunting, no hair pulling. Nothing but deafening silence.

Unable to wait for shit to happen, I lift my head and am rewarded with a back-handed slap across my face. It hurts, but I'd take the slap over the whipping any day.

"I said, say 'hello,' you stupid, fucking cunt," Sapphire yells. If I hadn't been able to see her, I'd have thought the devil himself had taken up residence in her body, she sounded that evil.

"No," I murmur and vigorously shake my head. I'm being stupid, I know, but I refuse to let them win.

"What did you say?" Stoner growls from his position against the wall.

"You heard me."

"Yeah and that's the goddamn problem."

Sapphire grabs me by the hair and drags me across the room, shoving me to the floor when we reach Stoner. I glance up at him, and now that I'm closer, I'm able to figure out how I know him. He's muscle for The White Lily. This just keeps getting better and better.

"So pretty." Stoner winks. "And stupid." He glances at Sapphire. "Any restrictions?"

Restrictions? What the hell is he talking about?

"No damage to the face." She tilts her head as if to remember any instructions she may have been given. She snaps her fingers. "Oh, and the pussy. No damage to that either. It is the money maker, after all."

"I can work with that."

Stoner reaches down, and when his fingers brush the skin at my collarbone, I snap out of it and lunge at him. I wrap a hand around his dick and squeeze, digging my nails into his flesh, and with my other hand, I twist his balls. Stoner screeches in pain and the sound sends satisfaction swimming through my system, but that satisfaction is short lived. Out of the corner of my eye, I see Sapphire's arm shoot out and feel the stab of a needle in my neck.

"Nooo," I howl, falling back on my ass as whatever she plunged into me swims through my system and threatens to take me under.

"Brandie!"

"No. No." I toss and turn, sweat covering my body like a second skin. "No."

"Brandie, wake up."

A warm hand settles on my arm, and I jackknife into a sitting position, my own arms flailing and my fist connecting with the face of my attacker.

"Jesus," he hisses. Strong arms wrap around my body, cradling me while also keeping me from striking out again. "Brandie, it's me. It's Slade."

I struggle against the man with the unforgiving arms, and after what feels like hours, his words finally slip through the veil of my nightmare fog.

Slade?

His arms loosen, and he leans back to look me in the eye, still holding me still by grasping my biceps. Concern swirls in his gaze, and I wince when I see the red mark from my punch.

"Brandie? You with me?"

I try to swallow past the lump in my throat, but I've got no saliva and it's almost impossible. Instead, I nod my head frantically and claw at my throat. Slade jumps up from the bed and rushes to the bathroom. He returns with a styrofoam cup of water, and I gulp it down greedily. When it's empty, I drop it onto the bed next to me.

"Thanks," I whisper.

"That must have been one hell of a nightmare."

"They always are." My eyes dart around the room, almost as if I'm reassuring myself that I'm not back in that underground hell. My eyes rest on his cheek, and I tip my head to indicate where he's going to have a nasty bruise. "Sorry about that. I didn't realize it was you."

"I know." The corners of his lips lift the tiniest bit. "You wanna talk about it?"

I scoot back and lean against the headboard. No, I don't want to talk about it, but I'm not going to be able to go back to sleep, so what the hell. Now is as good a time as any, I suppose. I pull my knees into my chest and wrap my arms around them.

"I tried to fight, to not let them break me." My voice cracks, and I take a few deep breaths to steady myself. "I think I could've handled them on their own, but Sapphire and Stoner together? I didn't stand a chance."

"There's not much anyone can do against pure evil."

Slade crawls up the mattress to rest against the headboard next to me. His legs are stretched out in front of him, crossed at the ankles. He's so close I can feel his body heat, but we're not touching. Without thinking, I lean my head on his shoulder, and after a moment's hesitation, he drapes an arm around me.

"Sapphire used a whip. I've got scars." My thoughts are scattered, disjointed. I realize I'm telling him things out of sequence, but I don't care. If I overthink it, I won't get anything out. "She said her father wanted me broken."

Slade's body tenses with each word that flows from my mouth. His heart beats wildly, in time with mine, and that comforts me.

"I lasted two days. That's all it took for them to get me to do what they want. Two fucking days."

"I know it doesn't feel like it, but that's a long time. Especially under those circumstances. Most don't last two hours. Hell, most don't make it out alive."

"I didn't want to. I wished they'd kill me. It would certainly have been easier than everything they did." I push myself away from his side and look him in the eyes. "I wasn't the only one, Slade. In the time I was there, I lost count of the number of girls they shuffled through. Some fought, some didn't. But every single one of them screamed."

Slade wipes away the tear that slips down my cheek with his thumb. He doesn't remove his hand when he's done.

"I am so sorry you had to go through any of that. I'm sorry that we didn't get you out sooner."

I shake my head and cover his hand with my own. "It's not your fault. It's their fault. That's one thing I've been able to work through in therapy. Every once in a while, the guilt that I couldn't save any of the others creeps in, but deep down, I know I wasn't responsible for what happened to them."

"Do you know any of their names?" he asks. Pain flashes across his features, and I can't imagine what it's like for him, as a person who is supposed to protect and serve. He's present with me, aware of me in the here and now, but he's also back in the office, flipping through files upon files of missing women who have families begging him to find their loved ones.

I shake my head. "The only one I ever saw was Katelyn. God, you can't imagine what it was like to see her standing there in that office. I was humiliated, ashamed, but also so happy to see her."

Slade lets his head fall back and blows out a sigh. "I wish we'd have gotten you out then."

"Honestly, me too. But, Slade, you did get me out."

"Right." There's a bite to his tone, an anger that doesn't feel directed at me. "Just not fast enough."

"We can go back and forth about this forever. Let's not. It happened. We can talk about it, you can ask questions, but I'm done playing the blame game. It doesn't help either of us, and it certainly isn't going to stop Sapphire from whatever the hell she's got planned."

Again, his body tenses as his gaze sharpens on me. His eyes are swimming with rage, and I know if given the opportunity to unleash it, he would be deadly. And a sense of power overwhelms me because, at least on some level, his rage is tied to me. It's there because of what happened to me, and his feelings toward my trauma go deeper than him just doing his job.

With that in mind, and with that newfound power coursing through me, I lean into him and capture his lips with mine. Slade's arms quickly wrap around me, pulling me closer. Flames ignite me from the inside out, licking my insides and turning me to a puddle of lust.

Slade's tongue glides past my lips, and I tangle mine with it. The sensual dance between our mouths is erotic and scary and far better than anything I've ever experienced or could have imagined. As the kiss continues to heat up, we paw at each other like animals. It's brutal, it's raw, it's fevered.

It's fucking perfect.

13

SLADE

"Slade." My body is shaking, and the fierce whisper is interrupting one hell of a dream. "Slade, c'mon. Wake up." I roll away from the annoyance. "Slade! Dammit, you need to see this."

Brandie's voice registers, and I'm instantly awake and aware that it's the real her, not the dream her.

"What? What happened?"

Without thinking, I grab the gun I stashed under the pillow after our make-out session. Things didn't go any further than she wanted, which left me with a set of blue balls and a smile. She'd asked me to sleep next to her, and I was happy to… more than happy. I knew sex was off the table, but just to be close to her, to have her *want* me close to her, that was everything.

"Your phone's been beeping like crazy." She's holding the cell out in front of her like it's a viper about to strike. Her eyes are wide, and her hand is shaking. "I wasn't snooping, I promise. It… it wouldn't stop so…"

A shudder rolls over her, and I snatch the phone from her and glance at the screen. My head feels as if it's going to explode at the text messages I see. There are dozens of them, but only one stands out and sends my fury into overdrive:

Unknown: You can run but you can't hide

"Grab your shit," I bark at Brandie. "We gotta get the hell outta here."

"Already ahead of you," she says.

When I glance at her, I realize what she means. Her bag is slung over her shoulder, and she's now standing close to the door. I shove my phone in my short's pocket and grab my own bag off the floor. We're both still dressed in the clothes we slept in, but we can stop later to change. Right now, it's not important.

I step out of the room ahead of her, scanning the parking lot and up and down the walkway. It's raining and there's a mist coming from the ground making it hard to see, but I'm as certain as I can be that there's no one lurking in the shadows.

Brandie's hand wraps in my T-shirt as we stride to the SUV, as if she's afraid she'll get

snatched en-route. I get her into the vehicle and rush around the front to get in the driver's side. I peel out of the parking lot and it's only when we hit the interstate that I realize we didn't check out. I shoot off a quick text to Jackson, filling him in and asking him to make the call to the motel. He responds with a short 'Will do. Call when you can.'.

I toss my phone into the center console and glance at Brandie out of the corner of my eye. My fingers grip the steering wheel so tight my knuckles are white.

"Are you okay?" I ask.

"Do you think she actually found us?"

I don't know the answer to that, but it's not likely. At least not yet. So I give her the best answer I can.

"I don't think so. If she had, it wouldn't have been a text that woke you up."

Brandie nods absently and wraps her arms around herself. It's warm out, but I turn the heat on anyway. She gives me a wan smile and reaches out to rest her hand on my arm.

"Thank you."

"For what?" I snort.

"For being there. For making sure I'm safe."

I let go of the wheel and grab her hand, bringing it to my lips.

"Always."

~

"Is it just me or has that car been—"

"Yeah, it's been following us for the last fifteen miles." My voice is gruff with frustration. I noticed the car almost immediately. I don't know what caused my suspicion, but the hair on the back of my neck stood up and my fears were confirmed when the vehicle followed every move I made. If I switch lanes, so do they. If I speed up or slow down, so do they. It's fucking infuriating.

"Do you think it's her?" Brandie continually looks over her shoulder, the fear in her eyes clear in the light shining through the car from the offending vehicle.

"Don't you?"

My eyes dart back and forth between the rearview mirror and the road. We've been driving for several hours and on very little sleep. We're both exhausted, but we can't stop now. Not with Sapphire likely on our tail.

"Grab my cell from the center console," I instruct Brandie. "Get Jackson on the phone. He's the second speed dial."

Brandie fumbles with the phone, and I know the second she sees who the first speed dial setting is for because I can feel her eyes burning a hole in my cheek when her head whips in my direction.

"I tried to get a hold of you. A lot." I shrug like it's no big deal that she's my number one contact. "It was quicker that way."

"Oh," she mumbles.

She puts the phone on speaker, and the ringing fills the car as I wait for Jackson to answer.

"What's up?" Jackson answers on the fifth ring.

"We've got a tail." I waste no time with pleasantries. "Not sure if it's Sapphire or not, but whoever the hell it is has been following us for a while."

"Can you shake them?"

"Not without some help." I shake my head even though he can't see me. "Think you could call the local police in…" I rattle off the name of the town I saw on the last road sign. "Maybe we can have her pulled over and this can all end here and now."

It's a long shot, but it would be nice to know that she's behind bars. If she's pulled over, surely she'd be arrested because they'd have to run her info and see all of BOLO's and such for her.

"Give me a few minutes and I'll call you back."

"Thanks, man."

"No problem."

The line goes dead, and I glance at Brandie as she sets the phone in her lap. She still looks scared, but her body doesn't appear as tense as it did a few minutes ago.

I pass the exit for the town I gave Jackson, and the vehicle still follows us. About five miles past that exit, red and blue lights flash in my rearview mirror, and the car pulls over. I use the time wisely and increase my speed to put as much distance between us and them as possible.

A sigh from Brandie fills the car, and I can't help but feel the same. Crisis averted. Danger over. I reach across the seat and pick her hand up in mine, bringing it to my lips and kissing her knuckles.

"Is it over?" she asks.

"I hope," I respond honestly. The truth is, I don't know if it's over. But I do know that, for now, we aren't being followed, and that means we're out of immediate danger. "Why don't you try to rest? I'm gonna drive for a few more hours."

"Okay. We're not that far away anyway. I think we should reach my apartment by nightfall."

I nod indicating that I heard her, but my mind whirls with thoughts. What if that wasn't Sapphire and she's waiting at Brandie's apartment? What if it was her and she catches up to us? What if it was Sapphire and she's arrested and the danger is over? Do I stay with Brandie, or do I leave this time and risk never seeing her again? So many questions and very little answers. Zero answers, in fact.

Brandie hands me my phone and then rests against the door and closes her eyes. It isn't long before her breathing evens out. I drum my fingers on my thigh as I drive and continue to torture myself with all of my unanswered questions.

Every few minutes, I glance at my phone as if doing so will make it ring. The next hour crawls by while the scenery outside of the car whizzes past as I barrel down the interstate. Finally, my phone rings and I'm grateful that I have it on vibrate so that it doesn't wake Brandie up.

"Please tell me we've got her," I answer after assuring myself that it's Jackson.

"All I can say is, when I was a sheriff, my department

never would have been such a cluster fuck." Jackson's voice is laced with venom.

"Jesus, what happened?" My gut is twisting into knots because now I have confirmation that the danger isn't over, even though I'm still waiting on Jackson to explain.

"The Chief of Police said that he sent an officer to pull the vehicle over, but the incompetent idiot didn't bother to run the ID or plates. Apparently, he took one look at the license and saw that it didn't say Sapphire on it and let the person go."

"Didn't you tell them how important this is? Didn't you—"

"Don't you dare blame this on me," Jackson snaps.

I take my hand off the steering wheel and shove my fingers through my hair, letting out a sigh as I do. He's right... he's not to blame.

"Sorry. This is just so goddamn frustrating."

"I get it. Trust me. But there's not much we can do about it at this point. They were doing us a favor by even pulling the car over. And who knows? Maybe it wasn't her."

"You don't believe that any more than I do."

It's Jackson's turn to sigh. "No. I don't. But it gave you the chance you needed to put some distance between you guys and her. Take the small victory and let's figure out what we do now."

"Now I get us to Brandie's apartment, and hopefully Sapphire strikes and we take her out."

"You mean we arrest her, right?" There's skepticism in Jackson's tone.

"Sure. That's what I meant."

"Slade, you can't—"

"Don't lecture me on what I can and can't do. You got what you needed with Kevin Vick. It's my turn." Brandie stirs in the passenger seat. "Listen, I gotta go. I'm gonna pull over somewhere and catch an hour or two of sleep and then drive the rest of the way. I'll let you know when we get to Brandie's apartment."

"Fine. Just be—"

I hit the end button, cutting Jackson off. I'm done talking, at least for now. I drive another forty miles before I see an exit sign that boasts a state park. Perfect place to park and get some sleep.

I follow the signs and pull into the park, flashing my federal ID at the gate so I don't have to pay. When I find an area where I can park and am mostly hidden, I shut the engine off and pull the lever to let the seat back.

I set my alarm on my phone for two hours from now and then keep the device gripped in my hand. Assuring myself that all the doors are locked and my gun is readily available, I lie back and stare at the ceiling of the car.

Before I know it, sleep pulls me under, and every worry temporarily vanishes.

14

BRANDIE

I stare out the window as Slade expertly maneuvers the vehicle to parallel park in front of my apartment building. I keep waiting for him to say something about how dumpy the building is or to criticize me for where I chose to live. He remains silent, and I'm so lost in thought that I don't even register that he's exited the car until he's standing on the other side of my window and he startles me by tapping on the glass.

"Nice place," he says when he opens my door.

"Don't hold back," I snap as I get out. "Tell me how you really feel."

A strong hand grips my shoulder while a much gentler one tips my chin up so I'm staring into Slade's eyes.

"Brandie, what's wrong?" Slade's voice is low, smooth.

"Nothing. I'd just appreciate it if you'd keep your scathing comments to yo—"

"What scathing comment?" He keeps his tone even. "All I said was 'nice place.'"

I roll my eyes at him. "That's not what you meant."

I fold my arms across my chest, and he drops his to his

sides. Both of us heave a sigh.

"You have no idea what I meant." His eyes never leave mine. "Sure, the neighborhood is rough, but—"

"I knew it!" I shout, cutting him off. "You're judging me."

"Oh for fuck's sake. I'm not judging you. It's a nice place. It's also likely all you could afford. I'm not stupid! I know you're used to more money than this place costs. Regardless of all that, I'm. Not. Judging. You." He takes a step back. "Why would I?"

"I don't know," I admit, injecting a bit of a pout into my tone.

I turn from him, and for the first time, realize we were arguing in the middle of the street. Slade has the ability to set me off like nothing I've ever experienced before. Not only that, but apparently, he can do it *and* make me forget where we are while he's at it.

"Brandie, you've got to stop jumping to conclusions."

"I don't know how. I can't help what comes out of my mouth sometimes."

Slade chuckles, and the sound washes over me, bringing with it an instant calm.

"What's so funny?"

"Nothing." He shakes his head. "Why don't we go inside and try to get some sleep? It's been a long few days, and I, for one, am exhausted."

I glance over my shoulder at my building and back at him, a thought suddenly occurring.

"I, uh, I only have one bed," I stammer.

"No big deal. I'll sleep on the couch."

Slade grips my bicep after slinging our bags over his shoulder and guides me inside. Once we're through the door, he slows down and allows me to take the lead since he doesn't know where we're going.

When we reach my door, I freeze. Nothing seems out of

place, but all I can think about is the last time I came to this door. The note that was waiting for me. The fear that slammed into me.

"Why don't you give me the key?" Slade puts his palm out for me, silently waiting while I dig in my purse. I place it in his hand, and when my fingertips graze his skin, a zing ricochets through my body. "Thanks. Just stay behind me."

"Why?"

"Because I want to make sure there's no one inside."

"Oh. Right."

Slade fits the key in the lock and pushes the door open. He keeps his hand on his gun, which sits in the holster at his hip. It takes him less than a minute to clear the apartment because it's so small.

We both stand in the kitchen, and I clear my throat. "Can I get you something to drink?"

"Sure. Whatever you've got is fine."

I open the refrigerator and realize I have nothing. I make a mental note to find time to go grocery shopping. Shutting the door, I slowly turn to face him.

"I've got tap water," I say and shrug when he raises a brow at me. "I haven't been here in a bit. We need to go to the store."

"We'll go tomorrow. And tap water is fine."

I grab a glass from the cupboard to the left of the sink and turn on the water to let it get cold. It takes longer than it should, but when the cup is full, I hand it to him.

"Thanks." He gulps the water down and sets the glass in the sink. "So…"

"So…"

The air seems to have been sucked from the tiny apartment, and my whole body tingles. From nerves or his close proximity, I have no idea.

"I'm going to call Jackson and let him know we're here,

and then I'm going to try to get some sleep, if that's okay."

"Absolutely. This is your show."

I take a step and try to pass him, but he stops me with a gentle touch.

"This isn't my show," he says softly, almost too softly. "Brandie, this is your home, not mine. Sure, I'm here to keep you safe, but make no mistake. I'm not running things as much as you think."

Unsure of what that means, I give a curt nod and head to the bathroom, where I close the door behind me and lean back against it. How can I be terrified of men, but inexplicably drawn to Slade at the same time?

I hear his voice through the wooden barrier and know that he's on the phone with Jackson. I take my time going through the motions of getting ready for bed. I forgot to grab pajamas, so I wrap myself up in my robe and tiptoe to my bedroom when I'm done.

I enter my room and stop in my tracks at the sight of Slade in his boxer briefs. I caught him changing. His back is to me, and if he heard me enter, he makes no indication of it. His muscles ripple as he digs through his bag that's sitting on my bed. I pray he's looking for a shirt to cover up all that temptation.

"I, uh, I'll come back," I say, but make no move to leave.

Slade whirls around at the sound of my voice, and his eyes narrow as his gaze travels up and down my body. The robe I put on is made of thin cotton, and I can feel my nipples pebble under his scrutiny, which means he can no doubt see the effect he's having on me.

"I'm almost done."

His voice is raspy, and he returns to digging through his bag. When he pulls a shirt out, he shoves his arms in the sleeves and tugs it down over his torso. An involuntary sigh escapes me when all that flesh is covered.

"Is that what you're wearing to bed?" he asks when he turns back around to face me.

"Um," I glance down at myself and try to swallow. "No. I forgot to take my clothes into the bathroom with me."

I slowly make my way to my dresser and open the top drawer to grab a pair of sleep shorts and a tank. A hand rests on my shoulder, and I shiver at the contact. When I close the drawer, Slade turns me around and our eyes lock.

He presses on my shoulders and leans down so his breath skitters across my ear. "I wasn't complaining." He kisses my cheek and steps back. "Get some sleep, Brandie."

I pull my lip between my teeth as Slade walks toward the door. Indecision rides me hard, and just as he steps through the doorway, I call out his name.

"Yo," he says as he glances over his shoulder.

"You could… Do you…" I heave a sigh and then spit out the words before I change my mind. "You can sleep in here if you want."

He slowly turns around to face me. "I'm not taking your bed from you. I'll be fine on the—"

"I meant *with* me."

Slade's eyes grow wide, and a grin spreads across his face. "Are you sure?"

I nod, unable to talk anymore. The thought of sleeping in the same bed with him has parts of me tingling that I thought were long dead.

I make no move to change into my shorts and tank, unsure of how to do that with him standing here staring at me. He seems to recognize my dilemma and clears his throat and strides back to his bag, pulling out his toothbrush and moving the bag to the floor.

"I'll be right back," he says as he holds it up and walks out of the room.

I release a breath I didn't know I was holding and rush to

change. By the time Slade returns, I'm curled up in the bed, as close to the wall as I can get, and the lights are off.

Air brushes my skin when he pulls the blanket back, and the mattress dips under his weight. The queen bed has always been just the right size, but suddenly, it feels too small. Slade scoots closer to me and rests a hand on my hip.

"Is this okay?" he asks.

I nod and then realize he can't see me. "Y-yes."

"Brandie?"

"Hmm?"

"G'night."

"Night."

I roll over so my back is to him, but then shimmy toward him so that we're spooning. There's no mistaking his sharp intake of breath the moment my ass makes contact, but I don't care. I may not trust myself, but I do trust him. In so much that I know he won't make a move if he thinks I don't want it.

When he makes no move to touch me at all, I reach behind me and grab his hand to pull his arm over me. He doesn't resist, and he lets me have complete control over where his hand rests.

My eyes drift closed, but I'm buzzing with sensation and I don't think I'll be able to sleep for a while. After several minutes, Slade's hand drifts under my tank and flattens on my stomach. My body tenses and I feel his head come closer to mine.

"Relax, Brandie. Nothing is going to happen. I just want to feel you."

It takes a few moments, but my muscles slowly relax, and when they do, his fingertips rub lazy circles around my belly button. It's not sexual, but it is soothing and within minutes, I drift off into the most peaceful sleep I've had in months.

15

SLADE

The alarm on my cell phone wakes me, and I roll over to turn it off. Light streams through the window in Brandie's room, and I make a mental note to get some blinds. When I roll back toward her, I freeze.

The blanket is down below her waist, and her tank has ridden up, leaving a clear view of the scars that criss cross over her back. Lash marks. I knew she had scars. I've caught glimpses of them when she's worn tanks to bed before. But I hadn't realized they covered her entire back.

My anger spikes at the sight, and not for the first time, I wish we'd have gotten her out sooner. I tentatively reach out and trace the raised flesh with my fingertips, each one a reminder of the hell she was put through.

Brandie stirs under my touch, but I don't stop. I know the instant she's fully awake because her shoulders stiffen and she pulls away from me.

"Don't," I plead and urge her back toward me. "Don't ever hide from me."

I continue to run my fingers over her back, and she slowly relaxes.

"They're ugly," she whispers.

That statement fuels my anger almost as much as the scars themselves do. I flatten my hand at her waist and tug her toward me. When her body aligns with mine, despite the bad timing, my dick jumps and I let out a chuckle.

"There's not a damn thing ugly about you." I thrust my hips a little. "Feel that?" She nods. "That's what you do to me. No matter how hard I try to not let you have that effect on me, you do. I lose that battle every single time."

Brandie sighs, and it seems as if the weight of the world is carried in that one breath. "You do the same to me."

"Give you a raging boner?"

The joke does what I intended, and Brandie snorts out a laugh. "Not quite."

"Good to know." I press my lips to a scar near her shoulder but don't linger. "We should probably get up and get our day started. We've got a lot to do."

"What's on the agenda today?" she asks.

We both get out of bed, and she tugs her tank down to cover her exposed skin as she stands. I'm barely able to contain the groan when she does.

"Well, we definitely need to go to the store. I'd also like you to take me to the diner where you work and—"

"Worked," she mumbles and fidgets with her hands.

"Huh?"

"The diner where I *worked*. I doubt I still have a job."

I think about her words, and I can't help but feel that may be a good thing. I hesitate a moment but say, "Maybe that's for the best."

Brandie's head whips up, and her eyes lock on mine. "How can that possibly be a good thing? I've got bills to pay. I've got rent, and I need to get a car, and—"

"You also need to stay alive," I growl as I close the distance between us. "Sapphire knows about the diner. You'd be a sitting duck there."

Her eyes spark fire. "Isn't that kinda the point? We came back here to draw her out and away from Katelyn. You know as well as I do that's not going to happen if I hole up in this damn apartment or never leave your side." Her arms spread wide, and then she drops them to her sides.

Dammit!

"I'll make you a deal," I start and when I'm sure she's paying attention, I continue. "Take me to the diner, let me get a feel for things, and we'll talk about it later."

"No deal." She shakes her head. "I'm a grown ass woman, Slade. I need to be able to make my own decisions."

"And you can," I counter. "But—"

"No 'buts'."

"*But*," I say as if she didn't interrupt me. "You need to let me keep you safe. I know you don't like it, but I need you to trust me."

"This has nothing to do with trust." She runs her fingers through her hair. "This is about me getting my life back."

"We're not going to get anywhere arguing. Let's just get ready to go and we'll talk about it later."

"Fine," she huffs and stalks past me out of the bedroom.

The bathroom door slams, causing me to flinch. I get her anger and frustration, and I'll even go so far as to say I'm glad to see the fire in her, but I won't risk her life, not for anything.

∾

"We can walk."

I toss my keys back on the kitchen counter. We just finished putting all of the groceries away and are getting ready to head to the diner.

"Did you always walk to work?" I ask.

She nods. "Don't have a car, so yeah." There's a defensive quality to her voice, but I choose to ignore it.

"Okay. Let's go."

As we walk to Chubby's Grub, I make sure I'm aware of our surroundings, at all times. It would be easy to get distracted by Brandie and the sway of her hips as she strolls slightly in front of me, but I don't let myself. It wouldn't do either of us any good, not right now.

"This is it." She points to the door but makes no move to open it.

"You okay?" I ask, sensing her apprehension.

"Yes. No." She shakes her head as if to rid herself of her confusion. "I don't know. I just left. What if they hate me?"

"No one could hate you."

"Tell that to Sapphire," she mumbles under her breath.

"You know what I meant."

I step around her and pull the door open. I watch her as she gathers her courage to step through, and when she does, her head is held high and a wide grin spreads across my face. *That's my girl.*

I follow her and scan the diner for any threats. Two men are walking toward Brandie, and I step in front of her.

"Where the hell have you been?" one of the guy's asks.

I'm immediately thrown off by his tone, but a glance over my shoulder tells me Brandie is unaffected.

"Nice to see some things don't change." Brandie takes a step and stands next to me. "Allen, this is Slade. Slade, this is Allen and his twin, Alex."

She makes the introductions, and I can't help but feel like Allen is sizing me up while Alex appears to not give a damn about my presence.

"Nice to meet you." I force the words past my lips and reach out my hand to shake each of theirs.

There's no mistaking the way Allen grips mine tighter than necessary. I don't know if Brandie knows it, but Allen definitely wants in her pants. Although, the way he's eye-fucking her, maybe he already has been.

Don't go there. You had—have—no real claim on her.

I hear a squeal behind me and look over my shoulder to see a woman practically dancing toward us. Her arms are spread wide, and she brushes past me to wrap them around Brandie.

"Girl, we've missed you," the woman says.

Brandie's eyes widen as if to say she has no idea why, but she returns the woman's hug. "I haven't been gone that long, Marilee."

Marilee steps back but keeps her hands on Brandie's biceps. "Maybe not, but the place just isn't as much fun without you."

"She's right, B."

I turn toward yet another voice and catch sight of an older gentleman with a hard look about him. He's smiling, but there's a shrewdness in his eyes, and it's clear he's sizing me up.

"Chubby..." Brandie turns toward him and drops her chin for a moment before squaring her shoulders and returning his stare. "I'm so sor—"

"Stop," he commands, and my hackles rise at his gruff tone. "Are you okay?"

Brandie looks confused for a moment before nodding. "Yeah. I'm good."

Chubby's gaze darts back and forth between Brandie and me as if trying to determine if there's truth in her words. Apparently, he's satisfied with what he sees because he takes a step toward her and wraps her in a hug.

"We missed you around here," he says. "Not the same without you."

The hug doesn't last long before he steps away and clears his throat. "Gotta get back to work. You've still got a job if you want it."

Brandie looks at me but says nothing. I make a split-second decision and give a curt nod. It's clear that she's made a life here and friends, even if she doesn't quite see it completely. Who am I to take that away from her? Besides, the way her face lights up at my response is enough for me to know I'd make the same decision over and over if it makes her smile like that.

"When do you want me to start?" Brandie asks Chubby.

"Tomorrow's soon enough." He turns to head back to the kitchen, but over his shoulder, he says, "Spend the rest of the day with your man and be here at six in the morning."

Neither of us correct him. I'm not her man, not yet. I sure as hell want to be though.

"You hungry?" I ask Brandie.

"Yeah. Where do you want to eat?"

"I was thinking here, if it's okay."

"You can have that booth," Marilee says as she points to a booth in the corner.

"Why don't you go sit? I need to talk to your boss for a minute." Brandie eyes me warily. "Trust me?"

She nods and Marilee threads her arms through Brandie's and leads her to the booth. I make my way to the kitchen and stop just inside the swinging door.

"Have a seat." Chubby doesn't bother to look at me, but he tilts his head to indicate the chair to my right. When I sit, he finally lifts his head. "That last day she was here, something was off. She asked to be walked home, which she never did. She was jumpy and on edge. I had Greg walk with her, and she never came back. I should've walked her myself."

I assess Chubby as he speaks, and it's clear that he blames

himself for whatever he thinks happened. While, like him, I wish he would've gone with her, I can't let him shoulder that.

"Has she told you anything about her life before she came here?" I ask. I need to figure out what he knows before I decide how to proceed.

"No." He shakes his head and then he pulls the sleeve of his greasy T-shirt up to expose a tattoo of the words 'Semper Fi' on his meaty bicep. "I'm not stupid, though." He drops the sleeve. "It was pretty clear she was running from something. Never gave too many details about her personal life, was thrilled to be paid cash under the table. She doesn't strike me as a rule breaker, so I figured if she was okay with scamming Uncle Sam, there was a reason."

"You don't miss much, do you?"

"Of course not," he huffs. "For instance, you've got a badge tucked in there somewhere." He nods to indicate my jacket. "And you fancy yourself in love with her."

"Brandie really wants to work." I choose not to address his assessment of me. I like Brandie, sure, but love? "I don't want to keep her from having a life, but I need to know she'll be safe while she's here."

"She'll be safe," Chubby says matter-of-factly. "She doesn't know it, but every time she left at the end of her shift, I watched her walk home. Every single time."

"Did something happen to make you feel you had to do that?"

"No." Chubby shakes his head. "Just my gut instincts telling me to keep an eye on her." He narrows his eyes at me. "Can you tell me what's going on, or is it some top-secret shit?"

I can't help but chuckle at him. He doesn't pull any punches, but I like him. More than that, I think I can trust him. I trust my gut instincts as much as he trusts his own.

"You ever watch the news?"

"'Course I do. Every night."

"National news or just local?"

"National. I didn't fight for this country just to ignore it when I got home." He sounds offended that I would even ask, but I don't apologize.

"Remember the story about a strip joint in Indianapolis? Two crime bosses?"

He tilts his head back and looks at the ceiling as if trying to recall details. When he lowers his gaze back to me, his eyes are wide. "Two guys named Vick and Luciano, right?"

I nod. "And one very dangerous daughter who is bent on revenge."

Chubby whistles through his teeth. "Damn. And Brandie is somehow involved?"

"I wouldn't say she's involved. She's one of their victims." I don't say anything more and watch as he seems to ponder my words.

He gives a sharp nod indicating he's put enough of the puzzle pieces together. "Maybe she shouldn't be working."

"You and I both know that if it's not here, it'll be somewhere else. At least here, she'll be relatively safe."

"Appreciate the vote of confidence. I promise I'll do everything I can to keep it."

"I know."

I stand to leave and join Brandie for some lunch. When my hand hits the door to push it open, Chubby's voice stops me.

"One more thing."

"What's that," I ask over my shoulder.

"I'll keep her safe. But that means from everything and *everyone*."

His meaning is clear. He may not be her father or even

what she would consider a close friend, but he's a stand-up guy and he gives a damn. I like him even more for it. I say the only thing I can to hopefully ease his mind where I'm concerned.

"Thank you."

16

BRANDIE

"If you insist on walking with me, you better get moving."

I stand by the front door of my apartment with my arms crossed over my chest and my foot tapping on the floor. It's my first day back to work and, despite my attitude, I'm grateful that Slade isn't going to let me go alone.

"Remind me again why you agreed to work this early?"

Slade has bitched about the early hour from the moment he woke up. I wasn't exactly thrilled to leave the bed either, considering I was curled up against warm, delicious man, but that's life.

"I took the shift offered. I'm not exactly in a position to argue with Chubby, now am I?"

"You're in a better position than you think."

"What's that supposed to mean?"

"Nothing," he mumbles. When his shoes are tied, he stands up straight, and I'm momentarily struck dumb at the sight of him. "Let's go."

I manage to unglue my feet and when Slade closes the door behind us, he sticks his key in the new lock he installed yesterday after lunch. The walk to the diner is uneventful. I can tell Slade wants to stick around, but after a shared look with Chubby, he leaves.

Within minutes of arriving, the breakfast crowd starts to show, and before I have a chance to wonder about the look, I'm swept up in work and keeping the customers happy. I'm clearing tables when I feel a hand on my shoulder, and it startles me so badly that I whirl around and drop the bin of dirty dishes I had resting on my hip.

The eyes of any remaining customers all focus on me, and heat creeps up my neck. Chubby races out of the kitchen and stops next to Allen, who is standing in front of me with his hands raised, palms out.

"What the hell?" Chubby glares at Allen.

I bend down to start picking up everything I dropped. "Sorry. I'll get it cleaned up."

"Brandie, stop." Chubby's voice carries an air of authority, and I stop what I'm doing and glance up to see him turn to Allen. "Since you caused this mess, you can help her clean it up."

"I'm a customer," Allen argues, sounding outraged. "You can't make me clean up her shit."

"Have you ordered any food today?" Chubby asks, and Allen shakes his head. "Did you come in here to order food?"

Allen looks at me and then returns his attention to Chubby. "Well, no, but—"

"But nothing," Chubby snaps. "You're not a customer today."

Allen huffs out a breath. Apparently, he's done arguing because he bends down to help me pick everything up. It takes a few minutes, and when I'm sure we've gotten all of the broken glass, I go grab the mop from the kitchen, not looking at Chubby as I do.

"Why are you here?" I ask Allen when I return.

An odd look comes across his face, but I dismiss it as frustration at having been forced to help me clean up.

"Can't a guy just stop by to say 'hi'?"

I study his face, his eyes, trying to find something, anything, that will tell me his motivations. I find nothing, which is exactly what I need to find my own strength.

"Ya know what?" I say and rest a hand on my cocked hip. "No. You can't stop by just to say 'hi'." His eyes narrow. "You've never done that before, so why now? Sure, you flirt like crazy, but I've got tips to make and bills to pay so I let it go. Well, I've got news for you. I'm done. No more flirting. I'm off the market."

It's not exactly a lie. Slade and I may not have made things between us official or put a label on it, but there's *something* there. Even if Slade didn't exist, I still wouldn't be interested in Allen. Not as anything other than a nuisance that comes with the job.

"You can't be serious," Allen argues. "Is it that guy that was here with you yesterday? It is, isn't it? You're fucking him."

"Who I choose to be with is none of your business. I'm not interested in you. Move on."

Allen's face contorts with rage. "You stupid bitch," he snarls.

"I really don't think you want to call her that."

I glance over Allen's shoulder and see Slade standing there, arms crossed over his chest. Allen slowly turns around and squares his shoulders.

"Oh no?" Allen challenges, and I immediately wince at his tone.

Allen has no idea what he's getting himself into with Slade. I don't imagine things will go well for him if he keeps it up. I step around him to stand between the two, but I face Allen.

"Allen, you should go."

He reaches his hand out, and I have no idea what he plans on doing, but there's no time to find out because Slade snakes his hand over my shoulder and grips Allen's wrist, twisting it. If it hurts, Allen makes no indication of it. Slade drags him toward the door, opens it, shoves Allen out and follows him.

I rush to the door and watch in fascination through the glass as Slade and Allen posture and yell at one another. I can't make out what they're saying because their words are muffled, but I have a feeling none of it's pretty.

"I like him."

I glance over my shoulder to see Chubby standing right behind me and Marilee next to him.

"Me too," Marilee says.

"Yeah," I sigh. "Me three."

After a few minutes, Allen stomps away and Slade comes back inside. He looks at me and then my boss and coworker and winks.

"Sorry. Had to take the trash out."

Chubby laughs and shakes his head as he returns to the kitchen. Marilee refocuses on the other customers remaining in the diner, and I just stand there, unsure of what to say.

"You okay?" Slade asks.

He rubs his hands up and down my arms, and I shiver. Watching him defend me stirred my hormones into a frenzy. My mouth is as dry as the desert making speech impossible, so I simply nod my head.

"Good." Slade drops his hands to his sides. "He shouldn't be back. But if he is, just let me know and I'll take care of it."

Wait. What?

My lust turns into frustration in two seconds flat. Despite evidence to the contrary, I *can* take care of myself. Especially when it comes to a stupid asshole who fancies himself God's gift to women.

"I don't need you to fight my battles." Slade opens his mouth to speak, but I hold my hand up to stop him from interrupting. "I appreciate what you did and what you do to keep me safe, but Allen's harmless." His eyes narrow, but I ignore it and continue. "Slade, you need to let me handle some things, some situations. How am I ever going to trust myself again if you fight all my battles?"

Slade's shoulders slump, and he releases a long breath. "Shit."

"C'mon, it's not that bad." I smile at him to lighten the mood. "You were just doing your job."

Something flashes in his eyes, but it's gone so quick I think I imagined it. "I wasn't doing my job." He takes a step toward me and brushes a strand of hair behind my ear. "Don't for one second think that I'm here because it's my job."

"Then wh—"

"Brandie, I'm here because I want to be here... with you."

On some level, I know this, but I'm still waiting for the other shoe to drop and Slade to tuck tail and run. It would certainly be easier for him. It's not like he can't track Sapphire from anywhere. At least if he weren't here, he wouldn't be in as much danger.

"I, uh, gotta get back to work." I turn to walk away but stop and face him again. "Did you need something? I wasn't expecting you until my shift was over."

"Right." He shoves his hand into his pocket, pulls out a cell phone and thrusts it at me. "I came to give you this. I got us both burners for emergencies. I don't want you to get rid of the phone you already have because we need to lure Sapphire out, but I also wanted you to have one that can't be traced."

I take the device. "Okay." I push it down into my back pocket. "Anything else?"

Slade shakes his head. "I'll be back when your shift is over."

I nod. "See ya later then."

Slade stares at me a moment longer before backing away. When he turns and walks out the door, I feel myself relax. Not because I'm glad he's gone but because any time he's near, I'm either tense or horny.

17

SLADE

"It's only been a week, man."

I thrust my fingers through my hair and let out a long sigh. Jackson and I have talked every day since Brandie and I arrived in Washington. Each day that passes brings with it more of a routine, and even though Sapphire hasn't made a move, just being with Brandie has been great.

"A week is a hell of a long time when you're cooped up with someone like Brandie."

"Ah, so your frustration isn't just the lack of progress on the case?"

"Fuck no," I say as I chuckle. "Look, I'm not going to sugarcoat this. You may be the only person to understand because of Katelyn." I take a deep breath and continue. "Sure, this started out as a need to protect a victim, but shit, now we might as well be living together as a couple. We sleep in the same bed. I get up to see her before work, and I walk home with her when her shift is over. We laugh and try to make things as normal as possible and—"

"So you two are in a relationship," Jackson states matter-of-factly.

"That's just it. I don't know what the hell we're doing. She's got the one thing I said I'd never want in a woman again, and that's baggage. Been there, done that and got the damn T-shirt. Divorce sucked, man. What if this is just some weird psychological bullshit because of the situation?"

"What if it's not?" Jackson's voice is so low I barely make out the words.

"The only way to figure that out is to end this shit."

"And that's where I come in."

A knot in my stomach forms at his tone. This is definitely going to be something I don't like, but it's probably also going to be something Jackson's right about.

"What do you have in mind?"

"We need to make Sapphire think Brandie's alone. Or at least ensure there are scenarios where it appears she is."

"I'm not setting Brandie up to be a sitting duck," I snap. "I didn't like the idea of her coming back here in the first place, and if you'll recall, I only agreed because I'd be here."

"Slade, you're not listening. I'm not saying she actually needs to be alone. We just need Sapphire to think that."

"And how do you propose we accomplish that? Sapphire isn't stupid. I'm sure she's watching us somehow, so she's going to see that I haven't really left."

"You've gotta stop going to the diner every day. Brandie needs to be seen alone... a lot. I know you won't agree to moving out of her apartment—"

"Damn right."

"And if you won't agree to that, then we need to figure something else out," he finishes as if I hadn't interrupted him. "Look, you said that her boss was a good guy, and you seem to trust him to watch over her. Trust him just a little more. That's all I'm asking. Give Sapphire a little more time each day to make a move."

"If she makes a move while Brandie's at work and I'm not

there, then what? I won't be there to catch Sapphire, and Brandie will get hurt."

This has got to be the dumbest idea Jackson has ever had. Funny how he can't see that when it doesn't affect the woman he loves.

"What do you suggest then? We've got nothing. We could always say 'fuck it' and you could come home, but then Sapphire is still out there and who knows how many others will get tangled up in her web of crazy."

"I've got nothing." I heave a sigh. "As much as I hate the waiting, I guess we just give it more time."

"Can you do that? Can you be cooped up with her and keep things professional?"

I bark out a laugh. "No, probably not. But hey, it worked out for you, right?"

"Speaking of, Katelyn has an ultrasound today, and we've gotta hit the road soon. One day at a time." He takes a deep breath. "At least try to keep it in your pants."

I agree to try, and we end the call. Noting the time, I grab my jacket off the back of the couch and head out to meet Brandie at the end of her shift.

As I walk to the diner, I think back over my conversation with Jackson. I recognize that he has a point as far as making Sapphire think Brandie's not being protected, but that doesn't mean I like it. I also recognize that the right thing to do would be to keep the relationship professional, but I don't like that either. I want more with her, regardless of how it all works out in the end. But there's some things she needs to know first.

When I enter the diner, Brandie is chatting with a customer in the corner booth. Her smile is genuine, and I'm glad I agreed to her coming back to work. She needs this, if for no other reason than to have as much normalcy as possible. Her happiness is worth every stress-filled minute I experience when she's out of my sight.

Brandie finishes what she's doing, and when she turns to walk to the kitchen, she catches sight of me, and for a second, that beautiful smile falters. She recovers quickly and shoves her pen behind her ear and her little notepad in the back pocket of her jeans.

"You're late," she says when she's standing in front of me.

I glance at my watch and note that I'm actually five minutes early. "Your shift ends at five. It's not five yet."

"Didn't you get my text?"

"What text?" I pull out my phone and bring up my messages. I have no missed texts from her, and I flip my phone around so she can see that for herself.

Brandie then pulls out her cell from her pocket and shows me the text she sent. "It's been a slow day, and Chubby said I could go home at three. When you didn't show, he sent Marilee home and kept me so I wouldn't be walking alone."

"I'm sorry. I would've been here earlier if I'd known." Why didn't I get her message? It makes no sense.

"It's fine. I can't leave yet though. I have to wait until Chrissy gets here now."

I can hear the frustration in her voice. She's been working all day, and she's likely tired. I nod and let her get back to whatever she needs to do and take a seat at a booth along the wall.

While I wait for her, I check all of my phone's settings to make sure nothing is off there. When I find nothing, I chalk up the failed text to a glitch and one time occurrence.

I watch my surroundings, taking in every person in the place and how they interact with Brandie. Much like I do every time I'm here. No one seems to be acting weird or *off*, and most of the customers are regulars I've seen numerous times. There is a gentleman at a table that doesn't look familiar, but his nose is buried in a newspaper, and I don't get a bad vibe from him.

Twenty minutes later, Chrissy rushes through the door, calling out apologies to Brandie and Chubby for being late. I remain seated because I know Brandie won't leave until her tables are cleared. It's another fifteen minutes before she's truly done, and when we leave, I find myself nervous.

"Other than the time mix-up, how was your day?" I ask after we've walked a block.

"Pretty good. I made good tips, which means more money for a vehicle."

She looks up at me and flashes a wide grin. I drape my arm across her shoulders and smile back. Not so long ago, she would have flinched at my touch or pulled away. Now, she leans into me and relaxes.

The remainder of the walk is silent except for the cars passing by, and when we reach Brandie's apartment building, she steps out from under my arm and stops moving. Her gaze darts up and down the street, and it's hard to miss the tiny shudder that racks her shoulders.

"What's wrong?" I ask when she makes no move to speak.

"I don't know. I just…" She fixes her gaze on my face and shakes her head. "Nothing. I'm being paranoid is all."

I rest my hands on her shoulders and stoop down to be at eye level with her. "Something spooked you. What was it?"

"Do you ever feel like you're being watched?"

I straighten to my full height and turn in a circle to see if I can pick out anything suspicious that could be the cause of her concern. Seeing nothing, I return my attention to her.

"Yeah, sometimes. I don't see anything that stands out to me, but I'm going to trust your gut."

I thread my fingers through hers and tug her inside so at least we're hidden from whatever, or whoever, may be outside sounding Brandie's internal alarm. We trudge up the stairwell and enter her apartment. She remains by the door while I do a quick sweep. It's our routine, and while she grumbled about it at first, she figured out pretty quickly that it's a routine I'm not willing to budge on.

"All good," I call as I exit the bedroom. "Why don't you go take a hot bath, and I'll get dinner ready?"

"That sounds perfect."

I watch Brandie strut to her room and enjoy the sway of her hips. I remain rooted in place until I hear the water turn on for her to fill the tub. Images of her naked body float through my mind, and my cock strains against my zipper.

Groaning, I adjust myself and make my way to the kitchen to make dinner. All I really want to do is order a pizza, but I'm not keen on the idea of having a stranger come to the door. I settle on making homemade pizza and am grateful we went grocery shopping and have everything we need. Brandie isn't big on a lot of toppings, and I like everything, so I compromise and stick to pepperoni and tons of cheese.

While the pizza bakes, I decide to check my phone settings and am able to determine that there is nothing wrong with them. That makes the mystery of the missed text all the more frustrating. I do a few online searches but come up empty on anything that leads me to the cause.

The oven timer beeps, and I take the pizza out to cool. I haven't heard the water drain or any movement from Brandie for that matter, so I knock on the bathroom door.

"Dinner's ready," I call through the barrier.

"Be out in a minute," she responds.

The sound of swishing water reaches my ears, and I imagine Brandie standing up and stepping over the tub's ledge, water cascading down her naked form. I lean against the wall and listen to the sounds coming from the bathroom, completely unaware of how much time is passing. When the door swings open and Brandie steps out in only a towel, she freezes.

My mouth goes dry, and my eyes drop to take in the swell of her breasts, the way they're heaving with her deep breaths. Next, I notice the pulse point at her throat beating rapidly, and it matches the rhythm of my own. Reaching out, I run my fingertip over her bare shoulder, tracing a path before wrapping them around the back of her neck.

I pull Brandie forward, stopping when our faces are mere inches apart. "I'm gonna kiss you," I rasp.

Her eyes grow round for a moment before she licks her lips and nods. I fuse my mouth to hers in a searing kiss, and heat seems to roll off of us in waves. Brandie moans and I thrust my free hand through her hair, being careful not to tug too hard.

Brandie's hands run up my chest and rest on my pecs. My libido is screaming for me to yank her towel off and have my way with her against the wall, but my brain is raging to slow things down. Almost as if the kiss has a mind of its own, it slows until we part and are both left panting.

"I, uh, I'm gonna go get dressed," Brandie stammers before turning and walking away.

I whirl around and retreat to the kitchen, my heart frantically slamming against my ribs. What the hell was I thinking, kissing her like that? It did nothing to ease my hunger for her. Quite the opposite. Now I want her more than ever.

As I set the food, paper plates and napkins on the coffee table, Brandie sits down on the couch. She put on a pair of cotton shorts and a tank top, exposing way too much flesh for my own good, and hints of the scars she carries with her every day.

"So," she starts after swallowing her first bite. "What's your story?"

I glance at her while I chew. When I'm able, I ask, "What do you mean?"

"You said you have a history that isn't all that great. I wanna know what it is."

This is the conversation I decided earlier to have tonight, but I certainly hadn't expected her to bring it up. I don't know if it makes it easier or not, but either way, my story could change her mind about a lot of things.

"Well, I was married before." Her eyes widen, and when her lips part like she's going to interrupt, I hold a hand up to stop her. "Let me get the basics out first. Please." Her lips press together. I know keeping silent isn't easy for her, so I appreciate the effort. "I've been married and divorced twice. Both times were my fault."

Rather than look disgusted, she looks curious. "Why do you say it was your fault?"

"I married women who I thought I could fix. Both had pretty shitty histories, bad luck with men." I give a self-deprecating laugh. "I was going to be the man to make everything better. Turns out, I was that man. But I was also not necessary for the long haul."

"Let me get this straight. You were exactly what they needed for a moment in time, and then they decided they didn't need you anymore, and you blame yourself for that?"

The way she sums my marriages up does make it sound less like the blame resides with me. "Okay, maybe you've got a point. Doesn't make relationships now any easier."

"All of that wouldn't matter if it's the right person. You need to find someone who makes you happy just as much as you make her happy. Not only that, but you can't be with a person who's only after what you can do for them."

"At least tell me you understand why all of this is haunting me now, under the current circumstances."

"I mean, yeah, I get it. You're worried that you only want

to be with me because you see me as someone who needs to be fixed. You're also worried that I like you because of what you can do for me, and the second I don't need your protection anymore, I'll be out."

"Let's get one thing clear," I say with a bite to my tone. "I don't see you as a project or someone who needs fixing. I see you as a woman who is incredibly strong and brave and will eventually realize you don't need me."

"Fair enough."

"So, where does that leave us?"

"Slade, I think it leaves us exactly where we are. Taking things one day at a time, one step at a time." She sets her paper plate on the coffee table. "But let me tell you something. That kiss earlier? I want more of that."

Instantly, my now calming heartbeat kicks back up a notch. "I think I can make that happen."

"It's no secret that I like you. A lot. I've just got a lot to work through still, but each day gets a little better than the last."

"I know. And you know you can talk to me about any of it, right?"

"I do. And I will. Soon."

"Fair enough."

I stand and carry the remnants of dinner to the kitchen, depositing most of it in the trash. When I return to the couch, Brandie is sitting cross-legged, but she jumps up before I have a chance to sit down.

"How about we get started on that whole 'more of that' thing?"

My mouth goes dry, and it's impossible to speak so I do the only other thing I can.

I kiss the hell out of her.

18

BRANDIE

"You're in control. All you have to do is tell me to stop."

Slade's words sneak their way into my foggy brain. We made out like teenagers in the living room and somehow found our way to the bedroom. We're both still clothed, and the heat between our bodies is intense.

I lay down on the bed and watch as he braces himself on outstretched arms to hover over me. I try to keep my hands to myself, but it's impossible. I start at his waist and run them up his torso before flattening them against his heartbeat.

"I don't want to stop." The words come out breathy.

Slade leans down and kisses me. It's not like it was in the living room. There's passion, but it's not primal. It's… sweet. And exactly what I need. With our mouths melded together, I work his T-shirt over his head, breaking apart only when absolutely necessary. At the same time, he works my tank top off. My nipples harden, almost painfully, when the cool air hits them.

Next I undo the button of his jeans and tug the zipper down. His lips move from my mouth to my chin and then down to my collar bone, where he nips and licks at my sensitive flesh. Shivers race down my spine as he works his magic.

Slade balances on one arm while he uses his free hand to shove my shorts over my hips. I lift my ass to help and kick my legs free of them. When I'm in only my green lace panties, he lifts himself up and lets his gaze travel the length of my body. My insides squirm under his scrutiny, and my heart flutters.

"This is hardly fair," I manage to say. "You should be naked."

"Is that what you want?" He quirks a brow at me.

I know he's giving me an out, a free pass to stop this in its tracks. I don't want a free pass. I want all of his deliciousness on display for me and only me. I nod.

He takes his time standing and shoving his jeans down to pool around his ankles. At least I think that's where they are. The second they cleared his hips, my eyes were glued to his jutting cock, completely unrestrained by clothes of any kind. We stay frozen in this state of awe of one another for what feels like long minutes but is probably only seconds.

"You are so goddamn beautiful."

Part of me wants to cover myself up, hide all of my imperfections. The rest of me wants to launch myself at him and wrap my body around his for eternity. I do neither.

The bed dips under his weight when he lays down beside me, and I roll over to face him. His left arm goes around me, and he traces the puckered flesh crisscrossing my back. I wince at the moment of contact, but his touch is so feather-light that I relax almost immediately.

"Badges of courage," he whispers. "Beautiful lines that tell your story."

"I don't like my story," I murmur, sounding almost intoxicated.

Slade rolls me to my stomach and straddles my thighs,

pinning me to the bed. Automatically, my muscles tense and anxiety threatens to overtake me. He leans over me, pressing his chest into my back, his rigid cock into my ass and wraps his arms around me, flattening his hands on my stomach. His warm breath glides over my ear, and I force myself to time my breathing with his.

"You okay?" I nod frantically. "Don't lie to me."

"I-I'm good," I push out.

Suddenly, his weight lifts off of me and is replaced by warm lips trailing fiery paths over my scars, down my back to the top of my panties. My hands fist in the sheets at the sensations he's evoking and moans crawl up my throat. His fingers find their way beneath the only remaining fabric on my body, and he yanks them down my thighs and legs.

I jump when his mouth presses against my ankle, and he reaches up to rest his hands on the backs of my thighs to hold me still. His tongue darts out and swirls around as he works his way back up.

When he reaches the globes of my ass, I think he's going to stop and flip me over, but he doesn't. Instead, he spreads my legs and licks my already wet pussy, causing me to tremble. One hand leaves a thigh and urges me to raise up on all fours. I oblige and am rewarded with a thick finger gliding into me while his tongue laps at my clit.

Without realizing it, my hips are thrusting toward his mouth, my body begging for release. Slade adds another finger, stretching me wider and filling me up. It's been so long since I've had anything physical feel good that my orgasm builds quickly, and when he crooks his fingers, hitting my G-spot, my limbs shake. He increases the pressure with his tongue, and in seconds, I'm flying over the edge, feeling destined to never return to Earth.

As the spasms slow and the trembling eases, Slade removes his fingers and slides down the bed, flipping me onto my back as he does. I'm spent and absolutely certain that I can't handle anything more. Then he crawls up my body and lowers himself on top of me. My core surges back to life, and I crave what I know he can give me.

"I need you," I say as I reach between us and fist his dick. "I need this inside of me."

Slade groans and slowly moves his hips. "I'm all yours."

I line his tip up and remove my hand so I can thrust my hips up and impale myself on him. The whole time, we're staring into each other's eyes, and when he slides into my wet heat, he groans. He holds himself still when he's buried balls deep.

"So fucking good."

"Move." I slowly pull back. "It feels better that way."

With his forearms braced on either side of my head, he does just that. He glides in and out. In and out. Each stroke is slow and precise, designed to devastate me, obliterate all conscious thought. I try to increase our speed, but he uses his hips to push back against my efforts and maintains his pace.

"Fuck me, Slade," I moan in his ear.

"Just trust me."

What he doesn't know is I do trust him. I trust him with my life, with my body. But do I trust him with my heart?

I wrap my arms around his neck and press my lips to his. Our tongues dance in perfect rhythm with our bodies. Slow, sensual, exquisite. I'm burning for him, with him. Pressure builds, pleasure ignites me from the inside out.

Each thrust in, Slade hits my clit and the friction is delicious. He mumbles incoherently against my lips and picks up the pace until he tenses. That one moment in time, when his hips freeze against my clit, and I explode around him, milking his cock. He pulses inside of me, and we both shout out our release.

Spent, sex-drunk and relaxed, we both collapse onto the

mattress. He manages to roll to his side and pull me into his arms. His heart beats erratically where my cheek is pressed into his chest, and I focus on it. He runs his fingertips up and down my arm, and goosebumps break out over my flesh.

"Cold?"

"No." I can hear the smile in my voice. "I'm perfect."

"Yeah. You are."

It isn't long before Slade's breathing evens out and his heartbeat slows. I'm too keyed up to sleep, so I enjoy the cocoon his arms provide. His confession about his failed marriages runs through my mind, but it doesn't scare me. In that moment, I realize that nothing about *him* scares me.

My judgement, or lack of, scares me. My ability to be what he deserves scares me. The threat looming over us scares the ever-loving hell out of me. But Slade doesn't. Not in the least.

Before sleep sucks me under, one last thought hits me. I *do* trust Slade with my heart.

～

"I'm so glad you answered."

Katelyn's voice comes through the line. I'm half asleep and I glance over my shoulder at Slade, still softly snoring and naked in my bed. I get out of bed and grab my robe off the dresser, throwing it on as I walk out to the living room.

"What are you doing up? It's so freaking early."

"Oh shit. I forgot, you're a few hours behind us." She sounds contrite, and I feel bad for asking. "I'm sorry."

"No, don't be sorry. I'm happy to talk to you." I plop down on the couch, curling my legs under me.

"Jackson just left for the office, so I figured I'd call. I hate not talking to you."

"Me too." I heave a sigh. I understand why the guys think

it's for the best that we don't talk, but I miss my best friend. "What's new there?"

"We're having a boy," she squeals, clearly unable to control her excitement.

"God, I wish I was there with you. I can't believe you're having a baby and I'm missing it. And a boy? I bet Jackson's over the moon."

"He is. We've known for a while, but this is the first chance I've had to call." She sniffles and I hate that she's sad. "And there's still time for you to be here for it. I mean, I'm only five and a half months along."

I can't tell if she really believes that the Sapphire shitstorm will be over in time, but I decide to roll with it. The thought of it not being over is too depressing.

"Right. I'll be back before we know it." Is that what I want? To go back to Indiana and leave the life I'm building in Washington behind? I don't know. "Anything else new?"

"Not really. Just getting fat and sticking close to home."

"Kate, I'm sure you look beautiful. Fat is so far from the truth."

"Tell that to my clothes." She chuckles. "Nothing fits anymore."

"You're pregnant. It's not supposed to fit."

"Yeah, yeah, yeah. So I've been told." I hear water running, and I imagine her making tea or something equally domestic. "You guys have any big plans for next week?"

Confused by the question, I search my brain for a reason we'd have plans. Coming up empty, I say, "Uh, no. Just the usual. Me going to work and Slade trying to figure out where Sapphire is. Why?"

"Slade didn't tell you?"

"Tell me what?"

"His birthday is next week."

"What?!" I shout and slap a hand over my mouth. I glance

toward the bedroom door and wait for any sign that I woke Slade up. After several seconds, when no sound comes, I lower my hand to my lap and play with the hem of my robe. "Why wouldn't he tell me that?"

"Maybe he forgot." The statement comes out more like a question. "I mean, he's got a lot on his mind."

"True," I concede. "Well, shit. I've gotta do something for him. He's done so much for me. Between keeping me safe and…"

"And what?" Katelyn asks when I don't finish.

A smile creeps over my face as I recall last night. "And other stuff."

"You slept with him, didn't you?"

There's no judgement in her tone, only a sense of amusement and wonder that only a best friend can provide.

"Girl, he's incredible. Whatever there is between us has been building for months, almost from the day he rescued me, and last night, well, it peaked. A few times." I giggle and so does she.

"Good for you. You deserve to be happy. He does make you happy, right?"

"Yeah, he does. I don't know how he does it, but he takes me out of my head. It's the little things, ya know? The way he holds me while we sleep. The way he wakes me up with a kiss to my cheek, and the way he walks me to work every morning and home with me every night. It's the way he's turned a shitty situation into something not so, well… shitty."

"I can relate. That's how it was with Jackson. I certainly didn't think we'd end up together like we are, about to have a baby. And I wouldn't trade it for anything."

"That's how I feel. I know we've been together under weird circumstances, but when I sit back and think about who I'd want by my side through it all, he's the only person that pops up. He's worried that when this is all over, there'll be nothing there, but I'm not so sure."

"Sounds like you love him."

Do I? Is that what this is? I've only been in love once in my life and it was my senior year of high school. Puppy love really. I don't know if I love Slade, but I do know I want to find out.

"Maybe." I take a deep breath. "Whatever it is, I want to see it through."

"Whatever you do, don't overthink it. Just let things happen and enjoy the ride."

"Oh, trust me, I enjoyed the ride."

The sound of a throat being cleared startles me, and I whip my head in the direction of the bedroom. Slade is leaning against the door frame with his arms crossed over his bare chest and a grin spread across his face. My gaze drops and takes in the fact that he's still completely naked.

"Gotta go," I mumble into the phone. "Love you, girl."

"Love you, too," Katelyn says as I end the call.

I rise from the couch and slowly make my way toward Slade. When I'm a few feet from him, he straightens and meets me.

"How much of that did you hear?" I swallow my embarrassment at having been caught.

"Enough." His grin widens.

"What's 'enough'?"

"Apparently, I make you happy and you enjoyed *the ride*."

Heat creeps up my cheeks. "You have a problem with that?" I challenge him.

"Nope."

"Good." I rise to my tiptoes and kiss him lightly. "I've gotta get ready for work."

I turn on my heel and head into the bathroom, shutting the door behind me. Slade's rumbling chuckle sounds from beyond the walls, and I laugh. His knock on the wood startles me, and I twist to open the door a crack.

"Yes?"

"Want some company?" He arches a brow.

"You plan on making me late for work?"

"Maybe."

I open the door further to allow him entry. He has me up against the wall within seconds and unties my robe. It falls to the floor, and he lifts me in his arms.

What follows does, indeed, make me late for work.

19

SLADE

"Jesus, I'm coming."

I abandon my laptop at the kitchen table and stride to the door. Brandie doesn't have a peep hole, so I don't have the luxury of checking out the visitor. Another knock sounds before my hand wraps around the knob.

When I throw open the barrier, I'm face to face with an older man in slacks and a polo shirt. He glances down at his phone and back up at me, confusion in his eyes. Shrewd eyes that cause my gut to twist.

"Is this Brandie Carlisle's apartment?" he asks, and his voice is familiar, but I can't quite place it.

"Who wants to know?" I demand.

"I'm Detective Lee. I'm following up on a case where she reported a suspicious note on her door."

I remember Brandie telling me that she hadn't gone to the police. Everything happened so quickly after she showed up on my doorstep that I'd completely forgotten about it until now. I know this guy isn't who he says he is, but I'm curious as to how far he'll take the charade, and I also want to see if he lets anything slip. Maybe this is the break we've been waiting for.

Besides, I've got my weapon tucked into my holster, and it's clearly visible. Surely he won't be stupid enough to try anything against an armed FBI agent.

"Sorry, detective." I thrust my hand out to shake his. "I'm Agent Cochran… Slade. We spoke on the phone a few weeks ago." He shakes my hand, and I note that his grip is sweaty. "Please, come in."

"Thanks."

'Detective Lee' steps around me and stands in the living room while I close and lock the door. I lead him to the table and push my laptop closed.

"Have a seat." His gaze darts around the apartment for a moment before he sits down. "Can I get you anything to drink?"

"No, no. I'm good."

I grab a bottled water out of the fridge and sit across from him. Aside from the shifty eyes and sweaty palms, this guy is good. I'll give him that. Time to put the pressure on.

"Can I see your badge, detective?" I make a point of chuckling. "Probably should have checked that at the door, but it slipped my mind."

He pulls a badge out of his pocket and slides it across the table. I pick it up and scan it. It looks legit, but I know it's not. More precisely, I hope it's not because if it is, he's a dirty cop. I slide the badge back to him.

"What can I do for you?"

"Like I said, I'm just following up. When we spoke before, neither of us knew where Ms. Carlisle was. I was in the neighborhood and thought I'd check in in case she returned."

"Any leads on who left the note?" I ask, knowing he has none.

"Uh, not yet. That's why I was hoping to talk to Ms.

Carlisle. Is she here?" He glances over his shoulder as if looking for her.

"No, she's not." I take a sip of my water, then glance behind me at the clock on the microwave. "Won't be home for a few hours."

"Oh, well…" He stands from his chair. "I'll just come by later."

"I don't really think there's a need to come back. She doesn't have any new information since speaking with your officers. And I'm here, so I'll make sure nothing happens to her."

His eye twitches, and I would have missed it had I not been watching him so closely. "How long are you in town for?"

I shrug. "Don't know." I decide to mess with him a bit. "A few days, maybe a week. Could be longer depending on how things go."

"Right." Eye twitch. "I see she's in good hands." He makes his way to the door, and I follow him. He hands me a business card, and I glance at it. *So, dirty cop.* "Please, have her give me a call. I'd like to talk with her one last time before I close the case since you're handling things."

"I'll do that, detective." He opens the door and crosses the threshold. "Thanks for stopping by." I close the door and flip the lock.

I immediately return to the table and snatch up my cell to place a call to Jackson.

"Hey," he answers on the third ring.

"I may have something. Can you run a name for me?" I could do it, but I want to see if Jackson picks up anything suspicious and comes to the same conclusion as I have.

"Hold on a sec. Let me grab a pen." The line is silent other than him rummaging through what I assume is his desk. "Okay, give me what you've got."

"The name is Detective Jeffrey Lee. That's Juliett, Echo, Foxtrot, Foxtrot, Romeo, Echo, Yankee and Lima, Echo, Echo."

"Got it. Is this the same detective that called you the night Brandie showed up on your doorstep?"

"It is. The thing is, Brandie swears she didn't go to the police at all with the note, so I'm not sure if he's even a detective. My gut says he is, but that he's dirty so I want a second pair of eyes on him."

"Shit. I hate dirty cops. For some reason, it'd sit better with me if he just isn't really who he says he is."

"You and me both. But his badge and business card look legit. I'll take a picture of the card and text it to you. If Sapphire has somehow managed to get a detective on her side, our job just got a little harder."

"Do you think she'd really do that? Take the risk of trying to lure a cop? Wouldn't she be worried about exposing herself to the law, especially if she didn't pick the right cop?"

"You'd think, but she's one crazy bitch. I don't think she plays by the same set of rules we're used to in most cases. I don't think we can rule anything out at this point."

"Jesus, when is this going to end? I do not want my son born into this shit."

"It'll be over before that. It has to be."

"Okay. Let me run that name, see what info I can dredge up and I'll get back to you."

"Sounds good. Thanks, man."

"Anytime. You know that."

We end the call, and I run a search of my own on the mysterious detective. I use Google while Jackson will use more official channels. I manage to pull up numerous articles hailing Jeffrey Lee as a hero and hot shot detective. Everything I read does not depict a cop on the take, but I'm reading information that's fed to the public. While it quells some of my suspicions, it doesn't douse them.

After an indeterminate amount of time searching the internet, I realize I've only got about an hour before Brandie's shift ends. I've got a surprise for her tonight, and I'm anxious to get on with it. I save a few of the articles to my desktop and shut down my laptop.

I take a quick shower and change into a clean pair of jeans and a blue Henley. I spray cologne and take one last look in the mirror before I grab a clean outfit for Brandie to change into and stuff it into a bag.

I lock the door behind me when I leave, and as I'm driving to the diner, my nerves kick into overdrive. I know that Brandie hates being stuck at home and has begged me many times to take her places. I've always resisted, but tonight, I'm caving into her wishes. There's a street fair in the next town over, and I did some checking. It usually draws enough of a crowd that it should be perfectly safe for us to go.

I park in front of the diner and make my way inside. Brandie is sitting on the counter, talking to Chubby. A quick glance around the place shows me why. The place is oddly empty for this time of day, and I have to wonder if this happens often.

"Finally," Brandie says as she hops off the counter when she spots me.

"Oh, it hasn't been that bad." Chubby laughs and walks toward me. "Your girl's been bitching all day about how slow it is. I tried to warn her it would be. Damn street fair always shuts us down for a few days. Happens every year."

"Screw the street fair. If I can't go, no one else should be able to," she pouts. "Besides, I could've used the tips. I'm so close to being able to get a car."

"I might have something to cheer you up." I toss the bag at her, and she catches it easily. "Go change."

She eyes me suspiciously and then opens the zipper to see the contents. She pulls out a pair of jeans and a long-sleeved black tee. "It's too hot for this."

"It'll cool off in a bit, as the sun starts to set. You'll be fine. I promise." I punctuate that with a wink.

Brandie groans but stomps off to the bathroom, I assume to do as she's told.

"Now just what do you have up your sleeve?" Chubby eyes me with the same suspicion as Brandie, except his eyes twinkle with it.

"I heard something about a street fair." I shrug. "She deserves some fun, don't ya think?"

"I do. It can get pretty rowdy, but it's usually teenagers blowing off some steam. You should be fine there."

"Thanks." I lift the hem of my shirt and flash my weapon. "We'll be good."

"Good man."

The bathroom door opens, and both Chubby and I turn to see Brandie walking back toward us. Chubby lets out a whistle, and I can only laugh. Normally that would make me jealous, but he's harmless where Brandie's concerned.

"Where are we going?" Brandie asks when she stops in front of me.

"You'll see."

I reach out and brush a strand of red hair behind her ear. Her eyelids flutter closed, and her lashes stand out against her skin. She put a bit of makeup on, and while she doesn't need it, she looks stunning. And that's in damn jeans and a tee.

Chubby clears his throat, and Brandie jumps back.

"You two have a good night. Brandie, why don't you take the day off tomorrow?"

"I need the money, though." I can tell she's thinking about it and is torn between wanting to take him up on his offer and wanting a vehicle so she can be less reliant on others.

"Fine. How 'bout this," Chubby says. "If you feel like coming in, great. If not, don't worry about it. We're going to be slow like today for a few days anyway. I can handle whatever stragglers we do get."

"Deal."

Brandie threads her fingers through mine and pulls me toward the door. We say our goodbyes to Chubby, quickly and over our shoulders because apparently, she's ready to find out what her surprise is.

She stops when she steps outside and sees the car. Her gaze darts to mine. "We're driving?"

"Yep."

I open the door for her and help her in. When I get settled into the driver's seat, I start the engine and pull out onto the street, pointing us in the direction of the fair.

"Are you sure this is okay?" she asks. "That we're going somewhere?"

"Let me worry about that, okay? If I didn't think it would be safe, we'd be going back to the apartment."

"Okay."

The parking lots for the fair are only about twenty miles away, and we're there in no time. Brandie's eyes light up when she sees the Ferris wheel, and she claps her hands like a little kid.

"Seriously? We're going to the fair?"

I reach out and grab her hand, bringing it to my lips to kiss her knuckles. "We are."

I pay the attendant the eight-dollar parking fee and find a spot in the middle of the lot, away from any trees or anything else that would provide cover for someone. Brandie and I hold hands as we walk toward the gate. My nerves slip away, and I allow myself to just be with her, enjoy the simplicity of the night.

"I can't believe you planned this."

We wait in line to pay for our tickets, and she settles against me, her back to my front. It would be so easy to lose myself in her, but I do manage to keep aware of our surroundings. When it's our turn, I pull out my wallet and hand over the cash. The second we step through the gate, Brandie pulls away from me and shoots off toward the food trucks.

It's on the tip of my tongue to call her back, warn her to be careful, but I don't. She's happy and having fun, and I don't have the heart to remind her about the other shit in our lives. She stops at a truck boasting Italian sausage sandwiches, and my mouth waters at the smell.

"This looks sooo good," she groans comically. "I'm starving."

"Never let it be said that I let you starve." I rest my hand on the small of her back, and we wait in yet another line.

After we eat, we walk around and take in everything. There are rides, food, games, vendors... you name it, it's at this street fair. We play a few games, and I even manage to win her a giant teddy bear. Then she wins another one and gives it to me. They're a pain in the ass to carry, but again, her smile is worth it.

I somehow convince the Ferris wheel attendant to hold onto our stuffed animals—okay, I slipped him a twenty—while we ride. At the top, Brandie rests her head on my shoulder and her hand on my thigh. My dick twitches, but I ignore it.

"Thank you," she whispers next to me.

"For what?"

"For making this the perfect night."

"Anytime."

20

BRANDIE

"We're home, babe."

Slade's hand shaking my shoulder and his deep voice register, and I lift my head from the window. I rub the sleep from my eyes and glance around. We're parked in front of my apartment building, and regret swamps me as I realize the night is over.

"I didn't mean to fall asleep," I mumble.

"It's fine. You were exhausted. It was a busy night."

Slade gets out of the car and walks around to open my door for me. I place my hand in his, and it feels like I'm being escorted to my front door at the end of a date. I guess it kinda is. The only difference is the guy won't be kissing me on my doorstep and driving away. I get to keep him. For now, anyway.

"What was your favorite part of the night?" he asks as we walk up the steps to my apartment.

"Mmm, it's a tie between the ice cream and the prizes we won."

"Shit, I left those in the car." He stops in the stairwell and turns to face me. "Stay right here, okay? I'll be right back."

He doesn't wait for my agreement before he jogs down the steps. Maybe it's the exhaustion or maybe it's the false sense of security I have after weeks of nothing, but I ascend the rest of the steps and walk down the hall to my apartment door. When I reach it, I realize the error in judgement.

There's a note on the door, exactly as there had been before, and the door is cracked open. With my heart in my throat, I whirl around and run back toward Slade. I'm halfway down the stairwell when I see him.

"What's wrong?" he demands after closing the distance between us two steps at a time.

"Th-there's a note." I point over my shoulder. "On the door. It's open. The door is open."

Slade drops the stuffed animals, and they roll back down the steps. Before I can even blink, he's got his gun drawn and is shoving his way past me.

"Stay behind me," he barks.

He's in full-on FBI mode, so I don't argue. Not that I'd want to.

When he reaches the door, he ignores the note and nudges it open with the toe of his boot. He steps inside and sweeps his gun back and forth as he checks the living room and kitchen. Apparently satisfied that there's no one there, he moves to the bathroom, which is the first door in the hallway. He clears that and then the bedroom. The entire time, I'm at his back, fighting the urge to wrap my fist in his shirt.

"It's clear." He turns and shoves his gun back in his holster before wrapping me in his arms and pressing a kiss to the top of my head. "You okay?"

I'm unable to talk because tears are threatening and my throat feels clogged. A shudder wracks my body, and he holds me tighter. After a few minutes, my trembling stops and he steps away.

"C'mon."

He tugs me with him back to the door and carefully pulls the knife out to release the note. Unlike the first one, it's longer, but it's written in the same blood-red marker as the original.

The street fair was pretty ballsy. Do you really think I've forgotten about you? Don't worry, I haven't.

"Goddammit!" Slade roars as he balls the note up and throws it to the floor.

He slams the door shut, flips the lock and starts to pace. He alternates between muttering incoherently and swearing viciously. I track his movement as dozens of questions filter through my brain. I ask the first one I can put voice to.

"She was there tonight? At the fair?"

He stops pacing in front of me and tilts my chin up to look at him. "Even if she wasn't, she somehow knew we were there." His eyes narrow. "The only person I told that we were going was Chubby."

"You think he's got something to do with her?"

He appears to think about it for a minute and then shakes his head. "No, I don't." He heaves a sigh. "If she was there, she had someone leave that note. If she left the note, she's got someone tailing us. Either way, I don't like it."

"That makes two of us."

"You know I won't let anything happen to you. I promise I'll keep you safe."

"Slade, that's not a promise you can make." When he opens his mouth to protest, I flatten my hand against his lips. "Hear me out." I remove my hand when I feel his lips press together. "I know that you'll do everything in your power to keep me safe and bring her down, but you can't promise nothing bad will happen. Not really. I'm not always with you."

"Maybe you should quit your job. Chubby would understand."

"No." I shake my head. "I won't do that. I won't let that bitch win."

"That's what I figured." He sighs in resignation. "I do think you should take tomorrow off, though. Chubby already told you to."

"I don't know what that will accomplish, but okay. I can do that."

"Good. Then tomorrow, I'm teaching you how to shoot."

I rear back. "Wait, what?"

"You need to learn to shoot. I don't ever want you caught alone without a way to protect yourself."

"Can't I just get pepper spray or something?" I really don't want to carry a gun with me everywhere I go.

"Do you really think pepper spray is going to stop her?"

"Maybe," I say hopefully.

"No, you don't," he challenges. "Besides, why take the chance?"

"Fine," I huff out, and then another thought occurs to me. "What about a permit? Won't I need one to be able to carry it concealed?"

He waves his hand dismissively. "Don't worry about that. I'll have Jackson push one through."

"I guess I'm learning to shoot tomorrow."

"Uh huh." He wraps his fingers around the back of my neck and tugs me toward him. "But tonight, you're going to learn how I can make you forget all your troubles."

"Oh yeah?" I bat my eyelashes at him.

"Yes, ma'am."

He presses a quick kiss to my lips and then steps around me to double check that the door is locked. When he's sure, he practically drags me to the bedroom, kicking the door shut behind him.

I back up a step for every one he takes toward me and bump into the edge of the bed. Slade reaches out and yanks my shirt up over my head. He expertly unhooks my bra and drags it down my arms. When he bends and sucks a nipple into his mouth, my back arches, thrusting the pebbled flesh toward him.

My hands fist in his hair, and he groans when I tug on it. He moves to the other nipple, trailing a wet path between my breasts with his tongue as he does. I let go of his hair to unbutton my jeans and shove them, along with my panties, past my hips so they pool at my feet. I kick myself free from them and then shift my attention to his pants. I'm surprised when my hand is met with hard cock, and I thank all the gods that he doesn't always wear his boxer briefs.

I grip Slade's arms to pull him down to the mattress. The kiss is broken, and Slade catches himself so he doesn't crush me with his weight. He rises to his knees and pulls his shirt over his head, tossing it to the floor with my discarded clothes. When he's as naked as I am, he doesn't fall forward but rather remains on his knees and lets his gaze travel from my head, down my body and back up again.

"I could look at your forever and still never get my fill."

Before I can respond, he leans forward and captures my mouth with his. His tongue demands entry, and I part my lips for him. We kiss like two people starving for each other, and when some of his weight settles on top of me, I thrust my hips up to meet his body.

I plant my feet on the edge of the bed and let my knees fall, opening myself up to him. He runs a finger through my folds, and when it comes away wet, he lines his cock up and thrusts into me with no hesitation.

The first time Slade and I had sex was slow and sweet. This time, it's all raw power and primal. There's nothing sweet about it. Slade pistons in and out of my slick pussy, and when he reaches between our bodies and presses his thumb against my clit, I explode.

"Oh, fuck, shit, oh God," I wail as I spasm around his thick dick.

As I'm coming down from my high, Slade's body stiffens, and he empties himself inside of me. One last shudder and he collapses next to me, leaving me feeling satisfied. I roll to face him, and he drapes an arm over my hip.

"Is it always going to be this good?" I ask.

"Damn, I hope so," he chuckles. "But I'll settle for just knowing we're going to get the chance to find out."

I scoot closer to him and rest my head on his chest. "Me too."

Neither of us fall asleep right away, but we remain silent. I replay the events of the evening, from the street fair to the horrendous surprise waiting for us when we got home. Every moment flashes in my mind, and I smile at one particular memory.

"Slade?"

"Yeah?" he asks sleepily.

"The stuffed animals are still at the bottom of the steps."

He barks out a laugh, and I join him. We laugh so hard that both of us have tears running down our cheeks by the time we're done. And just like that, everything else melts away.

For this one moment in time, I'm not a victim, a survivor or a job. In this moment, he's not an FBI agent or my big bad protector.

In this moment, we're two people who love being together and having fun. We're two people who are taking a chance and damning the consequences.

21

SLADE

"Is this really necessary?"

Brandie's arms are stretched in front of her, the gun pointed at the target. She's been grumbling ever since we left the apartment, making her displeasure at having to learn how to shoot known.

"Yes, it is. Focus," I instruct from behind her.

"Do you think I'm going to be able to *focus* when I've got an actual human at the other end of this barrel?" she snaps.

I reach around her and urge her arms down so the weapon is pointed at the ground and step around to face her. I frame her face in my hands and give her a quick peck on the lips.

"Maybe not, but it's better than nothing."

"Pepper spray is better than nothing, too," she retorts.

"Just try it. Please."

"Fine."

I return to my spot behind her and watch as she raises the weapon and squeezes off a round. When I look at the target, I'm shocked to see that she's hit it at center-mass.

"Damn. That was great."

"It's not hard, Slade." She spins around to face me. "Not when it's a paper target. Point and shoot."

I chuckle at her over simplified explanation. "Maybe it's not hard for you, but most people can't even hit the damn paper their first time."

"Really?"

"Yeah, really. It took me a while to get comfortable with the weight of the gun in my hands and then figure out how to actually make the weapon work for me."

"Huh." She thrusts the gun at me. "Let me see what you've got."

That's when it hits me. Brandie is competitive. If I make this a game of sorts, she'll be all in because she can't resist a challenge. So that's what I do.

"How about we make a bet?"

"What kind of bet?" she asks, her tone full of skepticism.

"Over the next hour, we'll both take turns shooting. Whoever hits the target the least amount of times has to cook dinner."

She glances at the target and then back to me with a shit-eating grin on her face. She sticks her slender hand out for me to shake. "You're on."

We each take our turns, and when it's time for the last round, I'm ahead by four and feeling pretty good. I'm certain I'm going to win, meaning she's in charge of dinner. Not only that, but she's damn good at shooting. I'd never have guessed she'd never done it before if she hadn't told me.

I take my last turn and manage to hit center-mass only one out of six shots. I flip the safety, hand the gun to Brandie and switch out the targets so she's got a fresh one. She takes her position, and I'm feeling pretty good as she takes a few extra seconds to steady herself. I may have fucked up this last round, but there's still no way she'll win. She'd have to hit center-mass with every shot this round.

"Are you watching closely?" she asks over her shoulder.

I give her a thumbs up, and she returns her attention ahead. She squeezes off six rounds so fast that it's impossible to see right away how she did. I push the button to bring the target back toward us, and my jaw drops.

There's one ragged hole at center-mass. *Holy shit.* She managed to hit it with all six shots.

~

Brandie

I pull my bottom lip between my teeth when I see the target and glance at Slade. His eyes are wide, and if his eyebrows could touch his hairline, no doubt they would be.

"I like my steak medium rare," I say and can't hold back the laugh that escapes.

"I can't believe you beat me."

Slade holds the target out in front of him and stares at it as if by doing so he can change the outcome. I yank it from his hands and start folding the paper.

"What are you doing?"

"I'm keeping this shit. Proof that I'm better than you." I tuck the paper under my arm. "I'm still not crazy about the idea of having to carry a gun, but at least I know I can shoot."

"I know you're not, but I appreciate you humoring me." Slade wraps his arm around my waist. "Now we just need to actually get you a gun."

I let out a groan, and Slade chuckles at me. I'm not looking forward to this part, but then again, I wasn't looking forward to the shooting range, and it wasn't as bad as I expected.

"Do I get to pick it out?" I ask as we step through the door.

SLADE'S FALL

"If you want, sure."

Slade drives us to the nearest gun shop, and when we enter, he pulls out his credentials and shows them to the man behind the counter. The guy is overweight with shrewd eyes and a beard that is in desperate need of a trim.

"I was wondering when you were going to show." He thrusts his hand out. "I'm Jay."

Slade shakes his hand. "Slade. And this is Brandie," he says by way of introducing me.

"Right. The little lady that needs a gun." Jay turns around and grabs a piece of paper off of the printer behind him. When he turns back around, he slides it across the counter toward me. "Take a look at all of the info, ma'am, make sure everything is accurate." Jay returns his attention to Slade while I do as he instructed. "Your partner sent over the permit a few minutes ago."

"Perfect." Slade glances at me. "Everything good?"

There are a few details that aren't accurate, but rather than mention them, I hand the paper to Slade and let him look it over. I trust that they're wrong for a reason. If I'm wrong, he'll point them out. He glances through the document, nodding the entire time.

"Everything seems to be in order, Jay." He hands the permit to him. "Show us what ya got."

Jay starts setting guns on the counter, and I have no idea what I should be looking for. Slade comments on a few, and Jay puts those away. I'm drawn to the smaller ones that can be hidden in my purse, and I focus on those.

"See anything you like?" Slade asks.

"I mean, sure, that one's okay." I point to the one on the far left. "But it's ugly."

Both Slade and Jay laugh at that. "They aren't supposed to be pretty," Slade says.

"I get that, but," I glance up at the one with the pink grip in the cabinet behind the counter. "At least that one has a little color to it."

"Can we see that one, Jay?"

"Sure thing." Jay gets the gun out of the locked cabinet and sets it in front of me. "This is a perfect little starter for you."

"Do you have any other colors?" I ask. I'll settle for pink, but I'd rather have blue or teal or something.

"I've got a few more back in the safe. Let me go get them for you."

Slade and I wait while Jay disappears into the back. I pick up the gun to see how it feels in my hand, and I'm surprised by how much I like it. It's compact and light, which would be nice. It doesn't look intimidating, and while some may not like that because they want to scare their attacker, I don't want to feel intimidated by my own source of protection.

"Here we go." Jay sets the same model weapon on the counter: one with a chrome grip and one with a teal grip.

"I'll take that one," I say and point to the teal one.

"Are you sure?" Slade asks.

"I'm sure. If I have to have a gun, I'm gonna at least look good with it."

"You heard her," Slade says to Jay. "We'll take that one."

Jay rings up the purchase, and Slade pays him in cash. I try to argue, but he doesn't listen, and within ten minutes, we're leaving the shop.

"Make sure you tell Chubby you've got that."

I look over at Slade. "What if he says I can't have it?"

"He won't. But I also want him to be aware that it's in his place of business."

"Okay. I'll make sure I tell him."

"Now, are you ready for your steak?"

A giant grin spreads across my face. "More than ready."

22

SLADE

"Is there anything else I can do to help?"

Chubby stirs the pot of chili he's working on while I sit in the kitchen at the diner with him. I brought the latest note with me so I could gage his reaction to it. Not that I thought he was involved, but you can never be too careful. When he read the note, he appeared genuinely disturbed by it, which confirmed my thoughts.

"Just keep doing what you're doing, making sure she's safe while she's here."

"I can certainly do that." He tastes the chili and adds more spices. "You know, I fought for this country so that people wouldn't have to suffer through this kind of shit. Pisses me off that good people are usually the ones burned by the evil in the world."

"Evil has no filter, no prejudice with regards to its victims. Evil doesn't care what you look like, how much money you have, or where you're from. It just exists. I wouldn't have a job otherwise." I shove my fingers through my hair. "I'd gladly give up that job though if it meant that it didn't exist."

Assured that Chubby is on the up and up and will continue to protect Brandie, I leave the diner after reminding Brandie that I'll pick her up when her shift ends. While I wait for Jackson's phone call, I decide to head to the police station to see if I can get a minute of Detective Lee's time.

When I talked to Jackson yesterday, he still hadn't been able to pull much on the guy, reporting that most of the records were password protected and normal FBI channels weren't working. He did confirm that he's an actual detective so at least something is the truth. Jackson also said he has one of the agents that specializes in cyber-crime helping him and would likely have something today.

I arrive at the station and immediately note that it's chaotic and loud. Officers are mostly busy with either suspects or witnesses. It strikes me as odd and very unprofessional that interviews are taking place in full view of anyone who walks in and not in closed interrogation rooms. If this is how the precinct is run, no wonder they may have a traitor in their midst.

"Can I help you?"

I turn my attention to the officer sitting at the front desk. He looks young, fresh-faced and eager to please. Maybe he can tell me something. Not only that, but it's likely I can get more out of him than I can Detective Lee, if I'm reading this guy right.

"I don't know. Hopefully." I show him my badge, and when he sees that I'm FBI, his eyes light up. "I'm here following up on a case, but maybe you can answer a few questions first."

"Yes, sir, I can do that."

He sits a little straighter, and I note that his name tag reads Officer Hardy. I stick my hand out to shake his and am glad to see that his handshake doesn't match his newbie attitude. It's strong, firm, and it crosses my mind that he may just make it in this life.

"I'm Agent Cochran. I appreciate your time Officer Hardy."

"No problem, sir. Anything I can do to help."

"Good, good." I try to keep my tone a mix of professional and comfortable in order to keep the officer talking. I need to make him respect my authority but also feel important. I do that, and he'll give me whatever I want whether he means to or not. "I'm doing a little digging into a case that involves a young woman and seems very similar to a case one of your detectives is working on. I'm needing everything you have on the local case so I can compare notes."

"Do you have the case number?" I shake my head. "How about the victim's name or the name of the detective who's working the case?"

"I believe the detective's name is Lee. Victim's name would be either Beth or Brandie."

Officer Hardy begins typing and searching the records for what I'm requesting. Several times, his eyes narrow and his brow furrows, as if what he's seeing doesn't make sense.

"Hmm," he mumbles as he continues to read the screen in front of him.

"What?"

"I don't know. It's just weird. There's a case here under the name Beth slash Brandie, so I assume that's the one you're asking about, but I can't get into it. I've tried to get into several of Detective Lee's case files and am being denied access to most of them. The ones I am able to get into are so heavily redacted that I couldn't tell you any specifics."

"Are digital case files usually so difficult to look at?" It's not uncommon for there to be multiple steps to verify the identity of the person trying to access the records. My gut tells me that's not the issue here, though.

"Keep in mind, Agent, that I'm relatively new to the police force, but this is the first time I've encountered this." He finally looks up at me and is sporting a frustrated smile. "Hell, the first week I was here, they plopped me in front of a computer and had me doing nothing but looking at old cases so I could, according to them, get a feel for the types of cases and crimes they deal with. Not once during that entire week was there an issue, and I looked at a lot of case files."

"Is that right?"

"Yes, sir." Officer Hardy looks confused, and I feel bad for the guy. "Would you like me to call Detective Lee so you can speak to him directly about the case?"

"That won't be necessary. I'm guessing he's a pretty busy man if your station is any indication," I say, referencing the chaos around us.

"Probably." He shrugs. "I'm sorry I couldn't be of more help. But if you think of something else I can do, please, let me know."

"I'll do that." I shake his hand again. "Thanks for trying. I appreciate it."

I leave the police station feeling even more confused and angry than when I arrived. Why would all of the case files for one specific officer be that hard to check into? It makes no sense.

Unless someone is trying to hide something.

∼

"It's about time."

I've been waiting for Jackson's call, all sorts of different scenarios running through my mind.

"Sorry, it took longer than expected." He takes a deep breath. "You sitting down?"

"No." There's something in his tone that has my gut churning. "Should I be?"

"Well, that's up to you. But let's just say I wish I would've been when I got the report back from our cyber-crimes guy."

"Dammit, just spit it out. What did he find?" I start pacing Brandie's small living room.

"For starters, Detective Jeffrey Lee is relatively new to Washington. He transferred there from Indiana."

"Son of a bitch!" I plop down on the couch. Jackson was right, I should have been sitting. "What else?"

"There are so many records on this guy that were a pain in the ass to crack, apparently. Asshole's got his case files locked down so tight that it was hard for even the FBI."

"Tell me about it," I mutter.

"What?"

"Nothing." I sigh and run my fingers through my hair. "Tell me you've got more than he's from Indiana."

"I do. Seems we've hit the jackpot." The sound of papers shuffling comes through the line. "Jeffrey Lee was apparently adopted at birth. Biological parents are listed as fourteen-year-old Anna Lang and sixteen-year-old Saul Luciano."

"You've got to be fucking kidding me," I shout. "He's Sapphire's biological brother?"

"Half-brother, yes. Same dad, different mom." I swear viciously. "Aside from birth and adoption records, we were able to link Sapphire and her brother as recently as a week ago through phone records."

"Things still aren't quite adding up," I say. "Clearly, he's working with her, but why? How did she find him? Most people don't just get involved in human trafficking and shit. How did she convince him to help her?"

"She didn't have to. Saul did that on his own."

"You're going to have to elaborate because my head is spinning right now."

"Cyber was able to hack email accounts and found correspondence between Saul and son from as far back as eight years ago. It seems Saul managed to get Lee on board with promises of unlimited money and women. Lee wasn't too hard to crack. He's been a part of this since before Vick or Luciano was even on the FBI's radar."

"And now that daddy's in prison, brother and sister are picking up the torch and trying to re-establish themselves? Or is there another end game?"

"From what I can tell, Lee has made a name for himself as the detective that closes missing person's cases wherever he goes. Specifically, missing women who might otherwise go unnoticed. And he does that by reporting that the missing are found and sealing all records to prevent too much digging. Apparently, no one questions it too much because it boosts their closed-cases numbers."

"Why transfer to Washington? Couldn't he have just helped Sapphire this once from Indiana? He actually transferred, and we both know it won't be easy to simply transfer back once they consider Brandie's *case* closed."

"I don't know. But I have a theory, and you're not going to like it."

"I don't like any of this, so don't stop now."

"I think they're moving the entire operation to Washington. Think about it," Jackson urges. "Sapphire's name is tarnished in Indiana. Sure, she was found innocent, and she's got The White Lily, but she can hire someone to run the club and still reap the benefits while keeping her hands somewhat clean."

"Go on."

"When she caught up to Brandie there, she saw an opportunity. And then lured her brother there with promises of building their own empire. It's a whole new, untapped victim pool. And with Lee's case record, it was a no brainer to hire him in an area where the missing person's rate is sky high."

"Is their end game with Brandie to kill her to tie up loose ends from Indiana, or is it to abduct her so she becomes another 'solved' missing persons case and their first money maker?"

"Does it matter which? Either way, Brandie's effectively eliminated."

"So, how do we stop them? I can get to Lee, but it's going to be hard to take down the golden boy of missing persons cases. Are we any closer to figuring out where Sapphire is?"

"We've managed to track her to the Idaho-Washington border, but we lose her trail there. We'll keep working on it. In the meantime, watch your back… and Brandie's."

With that ominous warning, Jackson ends the call. I've still got plenty of time before Brandie is done with work, but that doesn't stop me from locking up the apartment and heading to the diner.

After that phone call with Jackson, I need to see for myself that she's there, that she's okay.

23

BRANDIE

"Ms. Carlisle, I'm Detective Garmen. Can I get a few minutes of your time?"

I stare at the man sitting in my section, sipping the coffee that Chrissy poured for him before her shift ended and she asked me to take the table. Friend or foe? I can't tell and that has my stomach in knots.

"I'm very busy, as you can see." I glance around the diner at the full booths, remembering what Slade told me about Detective Lee and worried that this detective could be on the wrong side of the law, too.

Play it cool. Don't show your fear.

Slade's instructions echo in my mind, over and over again.

"It won't take long. Surely you get a break at some point." He smiles, and while I'm sure he means it to be comforting, it's not. "I can wait."

Not wanting to drag this out, I slide into the padded booth across from him. "That won't be necessary. I can give you five minutes."

"As I said, this won't take long." The detective pulls a

small notebook out of his pocket, along with a pen. "I'm assisting in an investigation into several missing women across the state. It's my understanding that you are a victim of human trafficking and the alleged trafficker in that crime may be in the area. Is that correct?"

At the mention of my nightmare at the hands of the Luciano's, my muscles tense and my mouth goes dry. How the hell does this guy know all of this? I've never gone to the police here, and, as far as I know, Slade's only talked to the one detective.

Unable to speak around the mountain of cotton in my mouth, I nod.

"What makes you think this person is here?"

Oh, I don't know... maybe the fucking scary notes on my door? Or how about the fact that my boyfriend—holy shit, I'll have to sort that thought out later—is an FBI agent, and he believes it to be true, so I do too?

I don't say anything like that though. I'm not going to give him more than what he already has, just in case he's not on my side.

"Gut feeling." It comes out sounding more like a question, and I can only hope he doesn't hear it.

"So, you haven't seen them or anything?"

Them? How does he know it's a 'them' and not a 'he' or 'she'?

I pretend to think about his question for a moment and then shake my head. "Nope."

"It's my understanding that whoever victimized you has already had their day in court. Two defendants were acquitted of all charges and one of them is now deceased. Is that correct?"

My fear and frustration turn to white hot rage at his reminder that Sapphire and Stoner weren't found guilty and the way he almost sounds sympathetic to the two of them.

"This conversation is over," I snap as I flatten my plans on the Formica table and scoot out of the booth. "If you need anything else from me, you can go through my lawyer."

I don't have a lawyer, but he doesn't need to know that. As far as I'm concerned, I've done nothing wrong so why should I have one? Besides, lawyers are damn expensive.

"Ms. Carlisle, please, sit down," Detective Garmen urges. "I still have a lot of que—"

"I believe she said she was done."

I whirl around at the sound of Chubby's voice, and all I want to do is throw my arms around his neck and thank him for being here.

"And you are?" The detective raises a brow, and his tone is condescending.

"I run this joint. And while I appreciate that you have a job to do, I'm not going to sit back and watch you do it wrong." Chubby takes a step closer to the table. "Now, I believe she said she's done talking. If you want something to eat or a refill on your coffee, fine, but if you're going to push her with more questions, you can get the hell out."

Detective Garmen rises from the booth and tosses a twenty onto the table, the whole time, glaring at me. "Keep the change. Put it toward your new car."

He shoves past me, and before I can pick my jaw up off the floor, he disappears out the door. Meaty hands rest on my shoulders and urge me toward the kitchen. It feels as if my feet have a mind of their own because when I'm pushed down onto a chair, I have no idea how I got there.

"Brandie, I need you to snap out of it."

Chubby's voice registers, and I shake away the fog. When I look at him, he's on his cell phone talking to someone with urgency. He tosses the device onto the stainless-steel prep counter and kneels in front of me.

"Slade's on his way." I nod and swallow past the lump in

my throat. "I'm sending you home for the day. I'll get Marilee to come in early and finish out your shift."

"O-okay," I manage. "How does he know I'm saving for a car?"

Chubby stands up and heaves a sigh. "I don't know."

We wait for Slade to arrive in silence. My heart is finally back to some semblance of a normal rhythm but kicks back into overdrive when Slade bursts through the door to the kitchen.

"Are you okay?" he asks as he yanks me up from the chair and wraps his arms around me.

I nod into his chest. "Yeah."

"Do you remember the detective's name?"

I take a step back and look into Slade's eyes. "He said his name was Detective Garmen."

"Did he show you his credentials or a badge? Give you a business card?"

"No, nothing." I realize now that I should have asked for those things, but my focus had been answering as few questions as possible and getting him the hell out of here.

"Okay." Slade thrusts his fingers through his hair, mussing it as he does. "Tell me what he said. Start at the beginning and don't leave anything out."

I spend the next five minutes talking Slade through everything from the moment the detective came through the door to the moment he left. Slade maintains eye contact the entire time I'm talking, and his eyes seem to spark fire every few seconds. By the time I'm done, he's coiled tighter than a boa constrictor around its prey.

"How'd he know about you saving to get a vehicle?"

"No clue. I mean, I don't talk to anyone outside of these four walls and you. I haven't even been to see my therapist since we came back. Maybe it was a lucky guess?" I don't believe that any more than I expect Slade to. "It's not uncommon to save for a vehicle."

"No, it's not. It's still an odd comment if he's just guessing."

"Have you talked to anyone in your department? Maybe you've got a leak." Chubby directs the question at Slade.

Slade bristles at the implication. "There isn't a leak."

"Now don't go getting your panties in a bunch. It wasn't an accusation, merely a question."

"Sorry. You're right." Slade begins to pace. "I suppose there could be a leak on our end, but I really don't think that's the case. I just don't know what I'm missing."

"Why don't you start with checking into this Detective Garmen character? Make sure he's even who he says he is. Then go from there," Chubby suggests.

Slade nods and pulls out his burner phone. Based on the conversation that takes place, I'm certain he's talking to Jackson, and when he hangs up, he seems to have calmed down a little and tells Chubby and me that Jackson's going to look into things.

"That's all you can do at this point." Chubby returns to his post at the cooktop. "Now, take your girl home," He nods toward me. "She's done for the day."

"Thanks Chubby. I really appreciate your looking out for her."

"Don't thank me. I don't know that I didn't make things worse, but it got that prick out of here for the time being."

"Either way, thanks."

Chubby grunts out a 'welcome' and effectively shuts down the conversation by focusing on getting orders cooked and out to the customers.

"Did you need me to call Marilee?" I ask Chubby.

"Nah, I already sent her a text. She'll be here any minute."

"I'll stick around until she gets here."

I look at Slade, and he gives a curt nod indicating he's fine with that.

"Suit yourself. I think I can handle things for a few minutes, but if it makes you feel better, fine. Go check on all the customers if you insist on being stubborn."

I laugh at Chubby's gruff nature and head through the swinging door to do just that. Slade is on my heels and takes a seat at the same table Detective Garmen was at just inside the door.

Marilee arrives ten minutes later, and I leave her to handle everything from here. It's busy, but she's a good waitress and doesn't crack under pressure so I don't feel bad for leaving.

Slade threads his fingers through mine as we walk home, and heat flows from my hand to spread throughout my body. By the time we make it into my living room, my body is buzzing. Any time this man touches me, my nerve endings come alive.

"How do you do that?" I ask him while I strip so I can change into something more comfortable.

"Do what?"

I glance over my shoulder to see Slade leaning against the bedroom door frame. One ankle is crossed over the other, and his hands are shoved into his pockets. I allow myself a moment to take in the sight of him... all of him. He does the same to me, and I watch in fascination as his gaze dips lower to ogle the exposed parts of me and his cock strains against his zipper.

"Huh?"

Slade pushes off the wooden frame and stalks toward me. "You asked how I 'do that', and I was asking for clarification."

"Oh." When he leans forward and nibbles on my ear lobe, my knees go weak and I stare straight ahead, at the wall. "What were we talking about?"

"Never mind," he chuckles, pressing his front to my back.

Slade grabs the tank top I'm holding and drops it to the floor. Then he shoves my thong over my hips and down my legs. He nudges my legs apart with his foot, and I hear him drop to his knees. I feel his shoulders work their way through my legs, and I drop my head to see him turned around, so he's pressed against the bed and facing my throbbing pussy.

A bolt of electricity shoots through me when his tongue flattens against my clit and he spears me with two fingers. He growls and groans while he eats me like a starving man, and the vibrations intensify the sensations rocking my body.

In no time at all, I'm spasming around him, and when the aftershocks die down, Slade slips from between my legs and places a hand between my shoulder blades.

"Bend over," he growls as he pushes me forward. The sound of rustling clothes reaches my ears, as does the quiet thump of them hitting the floor. When Slade grips my hips, he commands, "Hold on."

My hands fist in the sheets, and Slade impales me in one hard, smooth stroke. His hips fly, and I urge mine back to meet him. Sweaty skin slapping against sweaty skin and frantic panting are the only sounds in the room until a second wave of sublime pleasure rolls through me.

"I'm, oh shit, I'm coming," I stammer.

Slade picks up his pace, and each thrust causes me to scoot forward, and I lose my grip. I manage to brace myself on my elbows and ride out the pounding I'm taking. When my arms are about to give out on me, Slade stiffens and I feel him pulse inside of me.

I push myself up to stand, and Slade's arms go around my waist to steady me.

"What were we talking about?" he whispers in my ear.

"No clue."

"Yeah, me either."

Slade steps away from me, and I instantly miss his heat. He turns me around and brushes an errant strand of hair out of my face. Something flashes in his eyes, and I can't quite identify it.

"What's wrong?"

"Nothing." His eyes don't meet mine, and I know he's holding something back.

"Don't lie to me. Not now."

"It's just… I didn't mean for that to happen."

Feeling like I've been struck in the face, I pull away from him. "You regret it?"

"Hell, no, I don't regret it."

"Then what did you mean?"

"Brandie, you've had a shitty day, and the second I have you alone, I practically jump you." He begins pacing the floor. "I'd planned on bringing you home and maybe spoiling you a bit, so you could relax. But then you started changing and I couldn't think straight."

"That's a bad thing?"

"I don't know." His tone screams frustration. "But I don't want you to think that's all I care about. Don't get me wrong, the sex is great but that's not what keeps me interested."

I grab his arm to stop him from wearing a hole in the floor and force him to look at me. "Can I admit something to you?"

"Of course. You can tell me anything."

"Earlier today, when I was talking to that detective, my mind was racing a mile a minute. And one word hit me like a ton of bricks."

"What word?"

I take a deep breath, and my cheeks puff out before I exhale. "'Boyfriend'. I thought of you as my boyfriend." It's my turn to pace. "I mean, I don't know why. It's not like we're in an actual relationship. And we're grown adults. What self-respecting adult thinks in terms of boyfriend and girlfriend? A couple, yeah. Two people dating, absolutely. But boyfriend?"

I refuse to look at him as I continue to pace. Once again, my mind is racing and I know I'm babbling, likely not making a lick of sense.

"I'm good with that," Slade says softly.

I stop in my tracks and whip my head in his direction. "What?"

"I'm good with that." He closes the miniscule distance between us. "I like that you think of us like that. And trust me, it's not one sided."

"It's not?"

"Hell, no. Brandie, when we're together, the world fades away and I can almost forget the shitstorm that landed us here. And when you're at work, I find myself doing a lot of minute counting until I can see you again. You make me feel… I don't know. Complete in a way I've never felt and certainly never saw coming."

Hearing his words echo my own feelings is like finding a pot of gold at the end of a never-ending rainbow. It's crazy to me how strongly I feel about him, about us. Especially considering the circumstances and short amount of time we've known each other. I'm still a little scared that this might be less than what we think, but I'm not afraid to do everything I can to find out.

I lift Slade's hand into mine and flatten it against my chest so he can feel my heart thumping wildly.

"Ditto."

24

SLADE

"I'm gonna grab a shower."

I'm so focused on my task that I only manage to grunt in response. I'm going back through the transcripts from the trial of Saul, Sapphire and Stoner, trying to determine if there are any clues there that would give me more information about Detective Lee.

Neither Jackson nor I were able to track down anything about Detective Garmen. The fact that he exists is as far as we've managed to get in the few hours since he disappeared from the diner. He's based out of a town on the other side of the state, and it's not likely that he would come see Brandie at the diner without calling first, but it's not impossible.

I hear the water turn on and imagine Brandie naked under the spray. I force the images from my mind so I can continue my research. If I have anything to say about it, there will be plenty of time to explore all of my fantasies. There isn't, however, a lot of time to gather information. Not before someone gets hurt.

I'm not able to find anything incriminating on Garmen. The man seems to have a solid career in law enforcement and has even earned several commendations based on his exemplary service. His social media accounts depict a husband and father of three who appears to be motivated by family. There are some candid vacation photos, along with others that show him to be a guy with a lot of friends with a strong bond. Shit, he's probably someone I'd hang out with under other circumstances.

Aside from all of that, what really convinces me that he's not the villain is the countless posts from people, men and women, thanking him for arresting them and getting them down the right path in life. The guy's a goddamn hero, even to the criminals he encounters.

Then what the hell was he doing at the diner?

Switching my focus to Detective Lee, I start going through his social media. Despite the fact that I've already done this, as has Jackson and his cyber buddy, I'm thinking there has to be something we all missed.

I'm so engrossed in what I'm doing that I don't hear the water turn off or the bathroom door open. I don't even know Brandie is near me until her gasp filters through my concentration.

I swivel in my chair to see her expression go from one of shock to one of fury. "What's wrong?" I ask, not sure what's got her pissed off.

She tips her head to indicate my laptop. "I wasn't expecting to see that asshole in my kitchen."

"Detective Lee? I didn't think you'd met him." My brow furrows as I try to recall if she had or not.

"I haven't met Lee." She shakes her head. "But that's Garmen."

"What?" My gaze darts back and forth between Brandie and the photo of Detective Lee on my laptop screen. I point at the image. "Babe, that's Detective Lee." I scroll up on the webpage so she can see the name at the top of the Facebook profile. "See?"

"I'm telling you, that's the guy that was in the diner this morning. And he introduced himself as Garmen."

"You're sure?"

"Yes," she hisses. "Dammit, Slade, it was just a few hours ago. But even if it wasn't, I'm not likely to forget the face of the man who makes me feel threatened."

Brandie turns on her heel, but before she can stomp away from me, I shove up from the chair and step around her to block her exit.

"Slade, get out of my way."

There's a warning quality to her voice, and it reminds me of all the times I had to duck out of the way of flying objects that she threw at me. A smile creeps over my face as I remember.

"I don't know what you think is so funny about all of this," she huffs.

"Nothing." I force my expression to neutralize. "There is nothing funny about any of this. I was just thinking about you throwing things at me."

Brandie crosses her arms over her chest and begins to tap her foot. I'm pushing buttons that don't need to be pushed right now, but damn, it feels good to see this fire in her. She continues to glare at me, but I don't budge. While I like this defiant spark, I'm not going to let her walk away just because she's angry.

"What does all of this mean?" she finally asks when it's clear I'm not letting her past me.

It takes a moment for me to backtrack to the original conversation. When it does click, my anger spikes and I clench my fists at my sides.

"I'm pretty sure it means that it wasn't Detective Garmen that came to the diner this morning. Look," I nudge her to sit in my vacated chair and, over her shoulder, I pull up the real Detective Garmen's social media account. "This is Detective Garmen." I point at the screen.

"Okay. But that's not who I talked to."

"I'm getting that." I switch the screen back to Detective Lee. "This is Lee, the one who says you reported that original note."

"I didn't report any—"

"I know." I rest my hands on her shoulders and feel her muscles relax under my touch. "I'm not saying you did. All I'm saying is he says you did." I shake my head, even though she can't see me. "Anyway, if what you're saying is true, then it was Detective Lee that came this morning, pretending to be someone else."

"But why?" She looks up at me over her shoulder.

"I don't know."

"You have to have an opinion at least. I mean, why do you *think* he did that?"

"If I had to guess, I'd say Detective Lee knew I wasn't there so I could identify him. He knew he'd never actually met you, so he felt comfortable pretending to be someone else. I assume it was a scare tactic but also a way for him to ask questions and see how much you actually know."

Brandie rests her elbows on the table and drops her head in her hands. "Is this ever going to end? It just keeps getting more and more complicated."

"It's going to end. I don't know when or how, but it will end. I promise."

"I'm just so tired, ya know?"

Brandie lifts her head and stands up to face me. When she slips her arms around my waist and presses her cheek to my chest, I bend to lift her in my arms.

"What are you doing?"

"I'm taking you to bed."

"Slade," she manages around a weak laugh. "I'm not in the mood for sex."

"That's good because neither am I. But I do want to lay down next to you and hold you. Make you feel safe, even if for a little while."

She presses her nose into the crook of my neck. "Okay."

Over the next hour, I lay next to Brandie and align my front to her back, spooning her. She fights sleep, her body jerking awake each time she's close to being completely sucked under. I whisper reassurances to her, and eventually, she goes limp and her breathing evens out.

I stay next to her even though I know I need to call Jackson and fill him in. I don't want her to wake up alone, so I need to be sure she's in a deep sleep. After what feels like a decent amount of time, I scoot out of the bed, being extra careful not to jostle her awake. When I'm about to walk through the doorway, Brandie groans and I glance back to see her roll over and curl into a ball, but she doesn't wake.

I release the breath I'd been holding and head into the living room, dialing Jackson's number as I go.

Time to get to work.

$\sim$

Brandie

"Do you hear that?"

I don't look at Sapphire. I don't have to. The sneer in her tone tells me all I need to know. She's pissed and this is going to be brutal. Her hand fists in my hair, and I almost don't feel the burn in my scalp as she yanks my head back. She's done it so many times that I'm becoming numb to the pain.

"I asked you a fucking question!"

If she's asking me if I hear the screams coming from the other rooms, of course I do. But I remain silent. It doesn't matter if I answer her or not because the outcome will be the same. The screams won't stop, and my own will be added to the mix.

"Ya know, I thought you were going to be one of the smart ones," Sapphire says in a conversational tone that sends shivers racing down my spine. I recognize this tone as the one she gets when the consequences are going to be at their worst. "I thought you'd break and do as you're told. Imagine my surprise when you turn out to be one of the dumbest of the bunch."

I bite the inside of my cheek to keep from engaging with her. Blood coats my tongue, and I manage to swallow it down.

Sapphire releases her grip on my hair and shoves me forward. "Get up," she commands. I do as I'm told, pain radiating through my body. "Face the wall."

I take the few steps toward the wall of my cell. Pressing my naked body against the cold concrete, I stretch my arms at my sides so she can shackle them.

"See, you can be a good girl when you want to be."

I find a freckle on my arm and focus on it. If I focus on that, maybe I won't feel the lashing. That's what I tell myself every single time. Sometimes it works and I'm able to pretend I'm somewhere else, but most of the time it doesn't.

Sapphire trails the leather of the whip up the back of my legs, over my ass, all the way up to my neck. The first time she did that, it tickled, and I laughed. Big mistake. There's no laughter coming from me now. Only sheer terror.

I wince at the sting of the whip as she cracks it across my back, and the wounds from yesterday are sliced open. Blood trickles down until I imagine it dripping off of me.

"You will obey your master," Sapphire says as she whips me for the second time.

"You will represent this empire the way you're taught."

Whip number three.

"You will set an example for the others."

Four.

"Their success or failure is a direct result of your actions."

Five.

"We own you."

Six.

"Think of us as a landlord of sorts, and you're the property. We'll rent you to tenants for a price, and you will make them feel like they're home."

Seven. Eight.

"And if you don't learn your role and your place? I'll burn you to the fucking ground!"

Nine. Ten.

Sweat mixes with blood, and I can't fight myself any longer. I struggle against the shackles and turn my head as far as it'll go so I'm staring right at her.

"No."

As if in slow motion, Sapphire's eyes widen a split second before she raises the hand holding the whip and swings it down on my back one last time. I wince and squeeze my eyes shut against the pain.

I'm assaulted by a wave of nausea and dizziness that I can't stave off. Footsteps echo off the walls, and then there's a thud followed by a splash of cold water against my legs. My wrists are freed from their restraints.

"Clean yourself up. You look and smell disgusting."

"Can you hear me? Brandie, c'mon."

"No," I mumble as I begin to fall to the floor. "Too tired."

"Brandie, wake up."

Something prevents me from slipping into unconsciousness, and I fight it. I want to pass out. Hell, I want to die. If it would get me out of this hellhole, I'm fine with it.

"Brandie!"

I bolt up with a start and slowly become aware of my

surroundings. No concrete walls. No blood or nasty buckets of water to bathe with. No Sapphire.

Slade's arms come around me, and he slowly rocks me in place. "I'm so sorry." I have no idea what he's apologizing for. Just as I'm about to ask, he continues. "I'm sorry I left you alone. I wasn't thinking."

I shake my head against his chest. "Not your fault."

"You haven't had a nightmare in a while, and I thought you'd be okay." He kisses the top of my head.

"It's okay. I think everything is just catching up to me."

Slade pulls me down with him, and we settle into the mattress. "I'm not leaving. You can sleep now."

A blanket comes over me as Slade tucks it and himself around me. It takes some time for me to completely relax, but when I do, I settle into a peaceful sleep with no more nightmares.

25

BRANDIE

"I can't just leave."

I glare at Greg, hoping to intimidate him into doing me this favor. It's Slade's birthday and I want to make it special, or at least as special as I can with limited time and transportation. I need to go to the grocery store, but I don't have a vehicle and I certainly don't want to go alone.

"You're way early, and you know it. Your shift doesn't even start for an hour."

"I know but I've got a test to study for, and I was going to do that." To make his point, Greg pulls a textbook from his bag and drops it on the counter. "I have to pass this test or I can't practice with the team."

"Please, Greg. I wouldn't ask if it wasn't important."

"What wouldn't you ask?"

I whirl around and see Chubby standing behind me with his brow quirked.

"It's Slade's birthday, and I need to go to the store. I want to surprise him with a cake, and I need to get him a card or something."

"I'm not sure that's such a good idea."

I slump down in the chair against the wall. "It doesn't matter anyway. Greg won't take me."

"It's not that I don't want to help," Greg mutters. "I just have to study."

"It's fine. I'll just ask Chrissy to take me when her shift ends." I don't like that idea, but Chrissy is better than no one.

"Listen, I'm not crazy about the idea, but I'll take you. Slade's a good guy."

I hop up from the chair. "You will? But what about the diner?"

Chubby looks at Greg. "It's slow out there, kid. Can you handle the kitchen for a bit, and I'll give you an hour break when I get back?"

Greg nods. "Yeah. As long as I get a chance to study, I can do that."

"Good." Chubby returns his attention to me. "Get your shit and let's go."

He walks toward the back door without waiting for me. Chubby parks behind the diner in the only space available. When I step outside, he's already got his little Chevy S-10 running, and I climb into the passenger seat.

"Thank you for this," I say as I buckle my seatbelt.

"Don't mention it." Chubby puts the truck in drive and pulls out of the alley. "But we're gonna make this quick. I don't need the wrath of Slade if I don't have you back before he's supposed to pick you up." Chubby glances at me while we sit at a stop sign. "How'd you get him to come late? Your shift was over."

"I text him and told him we were busy so I was staying late. He didn't get much sleep last night, so I think he was going to relax for a bit longer."

"No sleep, huh?" Chubby cackles at his insinuation.

"It's not what you think," I say with laughter in my voice. I know that Chubby knows most of my history. Slade told me he filled him in so he could watch out for me. "I, um, sometimes I have nightmares. Last night was a bad night."

I fidget with my hands in my lap and stare out the window at the houses as we pass. Trees go by in a blur, and I realize that I've got tears in my eyes. I wipe them away and take a deep breath.

"Brandie?" I look at Chubby and see his kind smile. "We all have our ghosts. Don't let yours haunt you forever."

"I'm trying," I assure him. "What are your ghosts?"

"Does it matter?" he asks.

"No, I guess it doesn't. But…"

"Spit it out, B."

"I'm here if you ever want to talk."

I reach out and rest my hand on his bicep. With his left hand, he lets go of the steering wheel and pats my hand. "Thank you."

"Ahh, new subject."

Chubby snorts out a laugh. "Okay. What kind of cake are you getting?"

"I'm thinking vanilla with whipped frosting. Slade isn't big into junk food, so I'm pretty sure he wouldn't want chocolate."

"Sounds good." He looks in his rearview mirror, and I feel the truck slow a little. "If there's any left over you'll have to bring me a—" Chubby pounds a fist into the steering wheel. "Son of a bitch!"

"What?" I look out the back window and see the red and blue flashing lights. "What the hell? You weren't doing anything wrong."

"I know." He pulls to the side of the road. "Grab the registration and insurance card out of the glovebox."

I do as he asks and hand them to him then look over my shoulder to see the unmarked black sedan. The windows are tinted, blocking my view of the inside. The driver's door opens and as if in slow motion, an officer steps out. My stomach bottoms out when I see who it is. Detective Garmen, or Lee, or whatever the hell his real name is.

"That's him," I whisper to Chubby.

"I know. He doesn't know that we know though, so just keep your mouth shut and we should be fine."

I focus my attention on the side mirror so I don't look at the detective and give anything away. Chubby rolls his window down and waits.

"How can I help you, detective?" Chubby's tone is calm and even.

"It's your lucky day because I'm here to help you."

"Oh yeah? How's that?"

Paper rustles and I still don't look. "Here, read this."

There's a few seconds of silence, and then an outraged Chubby shouts, "You've got to be kidding me? You're arresting her for suspicion of human trafficking?"

My head whips to the left, and my jaw drops. "You can't be serious," I argue. "I'm a victim. You can't possibly think that I—"

"It doesn't matter what I think. It matters what the prosecutor can prove and what the judge thinks." Detective Lee draws his weapon and points it at me. "Now, please, step out of the vehicle."

This can't be happening. All I wanted to do was get a damn cake and surprise Slade. He's going to get a surprise all right, and not a good one.

Chubby's gaze darts back and forth between me and the detective. The look in his eyes is shrewd, and he nods almost imperceptibly. He's telling me to listen and get out, but I can't for the life of me figure out why.

"Get out of the fucking vehicle, now!" The detective demands.

Feeling my world spin out of control and having no other

option, I open the passenger door. At the same time, I hear the driver's door open and the detective cry out in pain. I glance over my shoulder to see Chubby slamming the door against the detective, I assume to try and dislodge the gun from his hand.

Detective Lee disappears from view, and Chubby is able to open the door fully and get out. "Run," he shouts at me.

I hesitate. I don't want to leave him to deal with this on his own, but I also know that if Detective Lee gets me, I won't be going to a jail cell. No, I'll be taken to a completely different kind of hell.

I take off running, back in the direction we came from, past the sedan. A gunshot echoes in the air, and I stutter to a stop. Again, indecision ricochets through me, and that split second of thought is all it takes for me to notice the rear passenger door of the sedan open and my worst nightmare stepping out.

"We meet again." Sapphire's tone drips with delight and is a stark contrast to the weapon in her hand. "I've been waiting for this day for a long time."

Something hits me in the stomach, and my entire body seizes up. My legs give out and I fall, my head grazing a rock before crashing onto the side of the road.

My vision blurs, and the last thing I remember is a boot coming at me and pain exploding in my skull.

Then… nothing.

26

SLADE

"Chubby, slow down. Breathe."

My phone rang seconds ago and seeing Chubby's number caused my heart to skip a beat. He's trying to tell me something, but his breathing is so erratic and labored that it's almost impossible to understand him.

"... store... surprise... Brandie..." He wheezes and sputters a cough.

"What about Brandie? What the hell is going on?"

I grab my keys and holstered weapon off the table and rush out the door and down the stairwell to my car.

"... detective... shot... crazy chick..."

My blood runs cold. "Where are you?"

"Lumber." Cough. "Run..."

As I race down the street, going as fast as traffic will allow, I try to recall where Lumber Run road is. There is now nothing but silence on the other end of line, and I know that time is critical, not only for Brandie, but for Chubby.

Think... where the hell is that road?

I recall all of the words that Chubby was able to get out, and he said something about the store. Was he taking

Brandie to the store? There's only one big store in this town that I know of, and that's the grocery. I head in that direction, and my mind races with the possibility of what I'm going to find.

I see a truck up ahead, pulled off on the side of the road. The driver's door is open, and as I get closer, I see a body lying next to it. I slam on the brakes and skid to a halt just behind the truck. The vehicle behind me blares their horn as they swerve to avoid a collision.

I throw my own door open and rush to the body. Bile rises up the back of my throat when I see that it's Chubby. I bend down to check for a pulse and am relieved when I feel a faint thumping under my fingers.

"Hold on, Chubby." I dial 911. "I'm going to get you help."

The operator answers, and I explain the scene. She assures me an ambulance is on its way and asks me to wait on the phone until they get here.

"Listen, lady. I'm FBI and there's been an abduction. I can't wait. Just get them here and make sure this guy lives."

I end the call and rush back to my vehicle. I hate to leave Chubby, but I hear sirens in the distance and know that they'll get to him in time. They have to.

My next call is to Jackson, and when he answers, I waste no time.

"They got Brandie and shot Chubby. I need you to track Brandie's phone."

"Who got Brandie? What are you—"

"Just fucking do it!" I shout. "I don't have time to explain. Just turn on the tracking app on her phone. I'm driving, so I can't."

"Hold on a sec," Jackson says, and a lot of white noise comes through the line. It's several long minutes before he comes back. "Done. I've got her location tracking next to yours. Looks like she's about twenty miles ahead of you."

I press the accelerator closer to the floorboard. "Okay. Stay with me in case they change directions or something."

"Got it." Katelyn's voice sounds in the background, and I hear Jackson tell her everything is fine. "Please don't make a liar out of me."

"I'm working on it."

There's several minutes of silence before Jackson speaks again. "Goddammit!"

"What? Talk to me."

"They got on the interstate. Northbound."

"What's to the north? Where are they headed?"

"Looks like there's a whole lot of nothing."

"Which means they've got a secluded hideaway. Run a quick records search, see if anything pops."

"Already on it," he replies. "Wait, this looks promising."

"What is it?"

"There's a cabin that appears to be in Detective Lee's biological mother's name. Now that can't be a coincidence."

"Nope. Don't believe in them."

"I'd say that's where they're going. I've got it up on Google Earth and it's about as secluded as it gets. Nothing but forest for miles."

"Send the coordinates to my GPS. I'm about to bring hell down on these fuckers."

"Done."

"Thanks, man. I'm gonna go and get there. Keep your phone handy, just in case."

"I'll get you some backup. Our guys so you don't have to worry about who to trust."

"That'd be great. I'm not waiting on them though. I'm going in when I get there."

"I'd argue, but I know you won't listen. Get her out of there and get her home. Otherwise, we're both dead men."

I know he's referring to the wrath of Katelyn if Brandie

ends up dead. He chuckles in an attempt to ease the tension, but it doesn't work. I'm coiled as tight as I've ever been, and the only thing that will relax me is having Brandie in my arms… alive.

"One last thing," I bark into the phone before he can hang up. "Check on Chubby for me. The ambulance should have him at the hospital by now. It wasn't far from the scene."

"Consider it done. Be safe."

Jackson ends the call, and when I hear my cell beep indicating that the coordinates came through, I tap the screen and let the GPS do its job. While I continue to speed toward my destination, I think of Brandie.

I'm coming for you.

From the moment I laid eyes on her, I knew she was different. Even naked and beaten into submission, there was fire in her eyes. Once she knew she was safe, that fire seemed to light up her soul. Sure, it took a while, but when it happened, watch out. Brandie is a force of nature, and I know that, if she survives this, she'll dig deep and come out swinging.

My exit is coming up, and I slow down enough so I don't roll the car around the bend. Once the road straightens out again, I press the pedal all the way down so the speed matches the adrenaline pumping through my system.

My phone beeps again, and I see a text from Jackson. I glance at it and read the words 'Chubby's gonna make it'. Relief rushes through me, but it's short lived when I note that the turnoff for the cabin is less than a mile ahead.

I take the dirt road and am jostled around in my seat as I make my way over all of the ruts. There are fresh tire tracks, so I know Jackson sent me to the right place. The sun is starting to set, and I've had my headlights on, but I turn them off so I don't alert anyone to my presence.

After another two miles on the dirt road, I see a clearing

up ahead. I stop my car and decide to go the rest of the way on foot. I check my weapon and assure myself that it's loaded and ready. I also grab the loaded gun in my glove box just in case.

The walk is short, and when I get to the clearing, I see a black sedan parked in front of a primitive looking shack. I silently make my way to the vehicle and verify that it's empty. I glance at the cabin just in time to see Sapphire and Detective Lee step outside.

They're shouting at each other, and I crouch down so I can listen.

"I could lose my job over this!"

"You're not going to lose your damn job," Sapphire yells. "You're the best they've got, and they know it. This is just a little setback."

"The woman on the floor in there is more than a setback," he argues.

My gut tightens at the mention of their captive. I've no doubt it's Brandie, and their words give me no indication of whether she's hurt or worse, dead.

"Trust me, she's not going to be any trouble." Sapphire is no longer yelling, and her tone turns matter of fact. "She's unconscious now, but even when she wakes up, I know how to keep her in line. We just have to keep her alive until Dad gets here. He'll know how to clean this mess up."

Dad? How the fuck is that gonna happen? He's behind bars in a maximum security prison.

"That could take days," Lee argues. "The paperwork was just sent this morning."

"Then we'll just have to keep her alive as long as it takes," Sapphire snaps.

"You said this was going to be better than Indiana. You said she was the key to it all and would make us rich. How is keeping her here and not selling her to the highest bidder not going to make us rich?"

"Shut up!" I shift positions so I can peer over the hood of the sedan and see Sapphire pacing. "Just shut the hell up before I lose it on *you!*"

"Go ahead," Lee challenges. "I'm your free pass, remember. With me, you stay out of prison. I die and I can't help you."

"No wonder Dad gave you up. You're a whiny fucker."

"Don't you dare…"

"What? Don't I dare, what?"

"Shut up," Lee snaps. "Did you hear that? I think she's awake."

Sapphire and Lee open the door, and that's when I make my move.

I take off toward the cabin, screaming, "Brandie, run!"

Both Sapphire and Lee look over their shoulders, and then it happens.

An explosion rocks the Earth. Pain and heat slam into me, lifting me off my feet and throwing me back through the air. I land on my back, and the breath is knocked from my lungs. A giant fireball and billowing clouds of black smoke obstruct my view so I'm not able to move out of the way before something heavy strikes me in the head, knocking me into oblivion.

27

BRANDIE

Fifteen minutes earlier...

A dull ache throbs in my muscles, and I roll my neck to take in my surroundings. I have no idea where I am, but the memory of a boot coming at me surfaces. I slowly raise my hand to the side of my head, and it comes away sticky with blood. *What the hell?*

There's shouting coming from somewhere, and I search for the source. There are shadows beyond the ragged curtains that hang over the windows. I strain to make out the words but can't. When I recognize the voices as those of Sapphire and Detective Lee, I groan. I don't remember there being anyone else but those two back at the truck, but what if I'm wrong?

I roll to my stomach and rise up on all fours. After assuring myself that I am, indeed, inside alone, I push past the pain and stand up. I somehow manage to remain upright, despite the dizziness that causes me to sway.

Turning in circles, I look for a way out. Sapphire and

SLADE'S FALL

Detective Lee are blocking my exit out the front, and I don't see any other doors.

Think, Brandie! There's gotta be a way out of this.

When the shouting stops, I drop to my knees behind the table and pray that I can't be spotted. I hold my breath for what feels like forever but is only seconds. My captors continue talking and when I'm sure that they're remaining outside, I continue my inspection of the cabin.

My eyes land on a propane tank and an idea begins to take shape. It's risky but it's all I've got. I look for the other items necessary to carry out my plan. I make note of the fact that the only light in the wooden structure is from a few lanterns and I determine that they're powered by oil and therefore, they have a flame.

Ignoring the agony, I manage to drag the propane tank closer to the table holding the lanterns and unscrew the safety nozzle. I know I don't have long to escape before the place blows, so I open a window and crawl out at the back of the cabin and take off running.

"Brandie, run!"

The sound of Slade's voice paralyzes me, and I skid to a stop, losing my balance and falling to the ground. My only plan had been to escape and kill the two that brought me here in the process. I hadn't known that Slade was here. If I'd known...

The explosion is so loud it drowns out my thoughts. I'm far enough away that it doesn't hurt me but close enough to feel the intensity of the heat. I scramble to my feet and break out into a run, back toward the destruction.

"Slade!" I scream his name, over and over, until my throat is raw from the smoke.

Sirens sound in the distance, and I assume they're coming this way, but I don't know for sure. I keep running, but it seems to take forever to reach the front of what used to be the cabin because I have to go around the devastation.

"Slade," I cry when I spot him.

I drop to my knees next to his limp body. He's covered in soot, and his clothes are torn. There's a large gash across the side of his head, and when I touch it, my fingers come away red and sticky.

"I'm so sorry," I wail. "I didn't know you were here. I'm so sorry."

I lift his head and place it in my lap. I press two fingers to his throat and am surprised by how hot his skin is. I'm equally surprised when I feel a pulse.

"Slade, c'mon. Stay with me." The sirens are getting louder. "Help is coming. You can't leave me like this. Please don't leave me," I beg.

Tears are streaming down my cheeks, mixing with ash as it continues to rain down on us. My flesh feels like it could melt off with the force of the heat at my back, but I don't care. I just want Slade to be okay.

"Ma'am." Someone touches my fingers at Slade's throat. "Ma'am, you have to let us help him."

"I'm not leaving him," I growl when a man tries to pull me away.

Chaos breaks out around me, but I'm only dimly aware of it. I feel myself being lifted off the ground, and I try to fight whoever is taking me away from Slade, but I'm not strong enough.

I look at the man who's carrying me and feel nothing. Not relief, not safe, not anything. I just want to be left alone with Slade.

"Ma'am, we're going to get you both to the hospital. You're going to be fine."

"Mmm," I mumble.

I'm placed on a gurney and loaded into the back of an ambulance. As another paramedic is hooking up my IV, I try to lift my head to look out the open doors. I'm not able to hold my head up long enough to see anything, but I hear people shouting orders and then another gurney is put in the ambulance next to mine.

"Go, go, go!" someone shouts as they slam the doors and the ambulance takes off with a jolt.

I reach my hand out and try to touch Slade, but he's too far.

"Slade," I murmur. "I'm right here. Slade, I'm here so you've gotta hold on. I'm so… so…"

A cold burn slithers through my veins, and my eyes drift closed just as an oxygen mask is placed over my mouth and nose.

∽

"Slow and easy, now."

As much as I want to argue with the nurse, I don't. My body aches, my head feels like it's being split open with an ax, my lungs burn, and my throat is on fire.

I wrap my lips around the straw sticking out of the pink plastic cup and take small sips. Cool liquid glides down my throat and eases it a bit. When the water is gone, I glance at the nurse.

"More," I croak.

"Just a little more and then that's enough for now."

She fills the cup and holds it for me to take another soothing drink. When she pulls it away, I let myself relax back against the pillows. The monitors surrounding me are beeping, and it's not helping my headache.

"So loud." The nurse taps on a few buttons, and the beeping sound lowers. "Thank you."

"You're welcome. Now, get some rest. I'll be back to check on you in a bit."

"Wait." I reach out and grab her arm to stop her from walking away.

"Yes?"

"The guy I came in with, is he okay?" Her face softens, and a look of pity flashes in her eyes. "No. No, no, no." I shake my head fiercely, ignoring the pain.

The nurse presses another button on the machine attached to my IV. I try to fight the drowsiness, but it's too difficult. I slip into sleep with visions of Slade's battered body in my lap and the knowledge that I did that to him.

The next time I wake up, the room is brighter, and I roll my neck so I can look out the window. The sun is shining, and it hurts my eyes. I let my lids fall and rest my arm over my eyes to block out the light.

"Oh, thank God."

I move my arm so fast, and my eyes blink open to see Katelyn standing next to my hospital bed. I open my mouth to speak, but nothing comes out. She gets me a drink of water, and it helps to soothe the ache and allows me to talk.

"What are you doing here?"

"You got blown up!" she shrieks, and I wince at the sound. "Sorry," she mutters. "But you got blown up, Brandie. You *and* Slade. Did you really think Jackson and I wouldn't come?"

"How long have I been out?"

"A while. We flew in yesterday as soon as Jackson got the call."

"Hi, sweetheart." Jackson steps up next to Katelyn and wraps his arms around her back. "How're you feeling?"

"You can't be here," I plead. Katelyn's face registers her hurt feelings, and Jackson opens his mouth to argue, but I stop him. "No, you can't. Because you being here makes it real, and it can't be real. He can't be gone. I love him, and he can't leave me. He promised he would protect me, and he can't if he's gone."

Jackson's hand rests on my knuckles, which are wrapped tightly around the bed rails. The nurse must have turned the sound back up because the machines beep wildly. "Brandie, stop. You're working yourself up."

Tears flow from my eyes, and I taste the salt from them when they hit my lips.

"Oh my God." I hear Katelyn's sharp intake of breath. "She thinks he's dead."

"Because he is," I wail.

"What?" Jackson focuses his attention on Katelyn. "Surely someone told her." He glances at me. "Well, damn. Sweetheart, Slade's alive."

Jackson's words register, and I glance at him. "But…"

"I promise. He's alive."

"But when I asked, the nurse wouldn't tell me anything. She just looked at me with pity, so I thought—"

"You thought he was dead," Katelyn finishes for me. She looks at Jackson, and her expression matches the one the nurse had.

"That," I accuse and point at her. "That's the look. What the hell is going on? What aren't you telling me?"

Jackson pulls his hand away from mine and thrusts his fingers through his hair, disheveling it. He takes a deep breath and quickly releases it. "He was conscious when he was brought in, but he suffered from several seizures." Katelyn grabs my hand while Jackson explains what happened. "After the last seizure, he was unconscious, and he hasn't woken up. The doctors are hopeful that he'll wake up once the trauma from the explosion and the seizures begins to heal, but they aren't sure if there will be brain damage."

"What do you mean there could be brain damage?"

"There's just no way for them to know how much his thought process, motor function and speech will be affected. Not until he wakes up."

"But he's going to wake up?"

"They believe so, yes," Katelyn says. "Slade's young and healthy. He's going to be fine."

"Can I see him?"

"We can ask the doctor if that's okay. Right now, they're being pretty strict about who can go in." Jackson smiles, but it doesn't quite reach his eyes. "They let me in because I'm FBI. I had to flash my badge to get them to, though. Katelyn hasn't been in to see him."

"I need to see him, Jackson." I reach out and grab his hand, squeezing tightly. "I need to tell him I'm sorry. I never meant for this to happen."

"I know, sweetheart. And he knows that. There's no way the blame could be placed on you."

"No, you don't understand." I shake my head and swallow past the lump in my throat. "I'm the one that blew up the cabin." Jackson's eyes grow comically round. "I was trying to save myself. I didn't know he was there. You have to believe me. I didn't know."

"Oh, Brandie," Katelyn cries as she sits next to me on the bed and tries to hold me. "Of course you didn't know. We know you wouldn't have hurt him. You love him."

"I really do. God, why is this happening? I finally have a great guy, the bad guys are dead, and now I screw up and Slade is paying the price."

"Uh, there's one more thing," Jackson says.

"What?" I groan.

"Sapphire is dead, but Detective Lee survived."

"Please tell me I at least injured him or he was arrested."

"He's definitely injured. He's already had several surgeries. He's also heavily guarded by police. Trust me. They're pissed as hell about what he's done and how he betrayed the badge. He's not going anywhere. They'll make sure of it."

I release a pent-up breath. "Okay. That's better than nothing, I guess."

"Listen, why don't you get some rest, and we'll come back to check on you in a bit?" Jackson suggests. "I've got to check in with the local suits and see where the investigation into your kidnapping and explosion stands. I also want to check in with Chubby and see—"

"Oh my God, Chubby!"

"He's fine. He's here in the hospital. He was shot, but the doctors were able to repair most of the damage. He should be going home in a few days."

"Thank God. Can I see him?"

"How about we bring him with us when we come by later?"

"That'd be great, thanks."

"Jackson," Katelyn starts. "I think I'm going to stay here with Brandie if that's okay. We've got a lot of catching up to do."

"That's fine, but don't forget, you've got more than just you to worry about." He nods at her very pregnant belly. "If you get tired, ask one of the nurses for a cot. If you're hungry, go to the cafeteria. Got it?"

"Yep. I'll be fine."

"Okay, then. I'm going to stop in and check on Slade before I leave, but I should be back in a few hours."

He bends down and gives Katelyn a kiss, and it's almost painful to watch because I want what they have. Just before he steps through the door, I call out to him.

"Jackson?"

"Yeah," he says over his shoulder.

"Tell Slade… tell him I…"

"I'll tell him."

28

SLADE

"Two weeks."

I stare at Jackson and try to process what he's told me several times already. Two weeks have passed since the explosion. Two weeks I've been lying in this bed while my body fought for life and my brain went offline. Two weeks without Brandie in the world.

I swallow around the lump in my throat. "That can't be right," I argue and glance around the room to see if my surroundings will tell me something different. "I didn't even get to tell her how I feel."

"You can tell her when she gets here." My eyes widen, and Jackson groans. "What is it with this place and them not telling anyone anything?" Jackson grumbles. "Brandie's fine. She had some bumps and bruises and had to be treated for smoke inhalation, but she was released the next day."

"But she was in the cabin when it exploded. They said—"

"Listen, I don't know what you heard, but she wasn't inside when the cabin blew." His forehead wrinkles with concern. "From what she says, she came to and realized she was alone. She rigged everything to blow and then jumped out a window. When the paramedics arrived, she was with you and had to be pulled away because she wouldn't let you go."

"She caused the explosion?"

"Yeah, she did." Jackson's tone sounds as if he's daring me to get pissed about that. He doesn't need to worry about it.

"Good for her." I manage a smile, but even that simple movement hurts.

"She didn't know you were there, Slade. She's beating herself up about that. A lot of guilt on her part."

"Why?" I ask incredulously. "I'm glad she did everything she could to escape. She's alive. I'm alive. That's all that matters."

"That's what I've tried to tell her, but she doesn't listen." Jackson shrugs. "She's convinced you're going to hate her."

"That's ridiculous. Why would I hate her?"

"Because I blew you up."

My head swivels toward the door. Brandie is standing there with a dejected look on her face and tears in her eyes. I can see her exhaustion in the circles under her eyes and the guilt in the way her shoulders slump. I've never been so happy to see someone in my life.

"Come here." I stretch my arm out, beckoning her to me.

Brandie shuffles her feet as she crosses the room. Katelyn is with her, but she remains by the door, and Jackson joins her. When Brandie is within reach, I wrap my fingers around her arm and pull her closer. I stare at her for long moments, and when she starts squirming under my scrutiny, I speak.

"Damn, it's good to see you."

Her head snaps up, and she finally looks me in the eyes.

"I thought you were dead," I push out. "But you're here. And you're okay."

A single tear slips from her eye, and she sniffles. "I'm so sorry. I never would have done—"

"Stop," I demand. Her lips press together. "The only people responsible for what happened are Sapphire and Detective Lee. I'm just glad we'll never have to worry about either of them again."

Brandie glances over her shoulder toward Jackson, and when her attention returns to me, she looks sadder than before.

"What? What am I missing?"

Jackson returns to stand next to the bed and clears his throat. "Detective Lee survived the blast."

"That's not possible," I argue. "He was standing right next to the cabin when it exploded. Both of them were."

"I don't know what to say. Sapphire didn't make it. Detective Lee did. Bastard got lucky."

"Where is he now?"

"He's still in the ICU but is heavily guarded. When the doctor's clear him medically, he'll be transferred to the jail to await trial."

"That's something, I guess." Another thought hits me. "What about Chubby?"

"He was released about a week ago," Brandie says. He's got a long road ahead of him with physical therapy, but he's going to be fine. He's already back at the diner. He's not cooking yet, but he's working Greg pretty hard."

"Good, good." There's something teasing my brain. I feel like there's something important that I'm forgetting, and I search my memory for it. I mentally run through the moments of the day, leading up to the explosion.

Walking to the clearing.

Seeing the empty sedan.

Listening to Sapphire and Detective Lee arguing about what to do with Brandie.

Sapphire yelling about her father.

Detective Lee saying something about orders taking time to process.

That's it! "What about Luciano? Please tell me his release paperwork didn't go through."

"He's still sitting in a cell where he belongs," Jackson assures me. "Fortunately, when the paperwork was received, the officer processing it remembered the media coverage of his trial and questioned the release order's validity."

I breathe a sigh of relief. Maybe this nightmare really is over. Maybe Brandie and I actually have a chance to figure out where we go from here. Glancing at her, I realize that's only going to happen if I can convince her that she's not to blame.

"Jackson, can we get a few minutes."

Jackson's eyes dart to Brandie, almost as if asking her if she's okay to be alone with me.

Anger rolls through me at what appears to be his desire to protect her… from me. Protecting her is not his job. It's mine.

Brandie nods and a growl escapes past my lips. Jackson and Katelyn hesitate a moment before leaving, and when they do, I focus all of my attention on the woman next to me.

"What's going through that head of yours?" I ask, trying to keep things light.

Brandie shrugs and looks everywhere but at me.

"Why won't you look at me?"

Again, she shrugs.

"Dammit, look at me," I bark. I take a deep breath. "Please."

Brandie's eyes lock on mine. "I thought I killed you," she mumbles.

"But you didn't. I'm right here." I grab her hand and squeeze. "Feel that?" She nods. "I'm alive, and I'm going to be fine."

"Slade, I'm scared."

"Of what? Me?"

"No." She sighs. "I'm afraid it isn't really over. I'm afraid that if it *is*, then so are we. I'm just scared."

"Brandie, it's really over," I assure her. "As over as it can be, anyway. I promise. And you know what else?"

"What?"

"We are definitely *not* over." Her eyes widen. "You heard me. When Chubby called me and told me you'd been taken, something inside of me snapped. I wasn't ready to give you up, so I found you. Then the cabin exploded, and I thought you were inside. As I was flying through the air, I remember thinking that I hoped the blast killed me. Because I didn't want to live in a world without you in it."

"What are you saying?"

"I'm saying that, while getting blown up isn't on my list of things to experience again, I'm glad it happened. I'm glad I lived because you lived. I'm saying that it confirmed what I've been feeling for a while." I rub circles over the back of her hand with my thumb. "I'm saying that I love you."

"But—"

"No 'buts'." I chuckle and shake my head. "You are the most stubborn, hard-headed woman I've ever met. I tell you I love you, and you want to argue." Brandie's face turns a pretty shade of pink. "Let me ask you something."

"Okay."

"When you thought you'd killed me, what was the first thing that went through your head?"

"That I didn't even get a chance to tell you how I felt about you."

"And how did you feel about me?"

"I loved you. At that moment, I knew I loved you."

"Do you feel the same way right now?"

"Of course."

"Then why can't you accept the fact that I love you too? That we can be together without all the other bullshit taking up space? Either you love me, or you don't. Either you want to be with me, or you don't."

"I love you. I want to be with you," she insists.

"Then just let it be. Other than the lack of a threat, nothing changes. We still take things one day at a time and love each other the best we know how."

"You make it sound so simple."

"That's because it is." I reach up and wrap my fingers around the back of her neck to pull her in for a kiss. When we break apart, I gaze into her eyes and see her soul reflected there. "Loving you is the simplest thing I've ever done."

EPILOGUE

BRANDIE

Four months later...

"I miss you so much."

Katelyn sounds sleepy, and I can only imagine how exhausting being a new mom is. She's a natural though. Even from across the country, I can tell.

"I miss you, too."

I glance at the framed photo of her holding her son the day they came home from the hospital. I wish I could have been there, but until yesterday, Slade and I were dealing with Detective Lee's trial.

"Now that everything is done, are you two going to come for a few days?" Katelyn asks.

"Absolutely. I think we're planning on next week sometime. After we get everything situated at the new place."

"Speaking of, when are you actually moving?"

"Slade's picking up the truck now so we can clear out the apartment. I'm just finishing up last minute packing."

"Can you believe how things worked out? Just over a year ago, we were both in hell, and now look at us. I'm a mom and you're settling down with the man of your dreams."

"Tell me about it. I wish that neither of us had to go through what we went through, but I'm glad it brought us to where we are now. It makes all the suffering worth it."

"It does." A piercing cry comes through the line. "That's my cue," Katelyn laughs. "Let me know when you get your plane tickets and flight information, and we'll pick you guys up at the airport."

"Sounds good. Talk to you soon."

I end the call and shove my phone into my back pocket. I continue packing boxes, the entire time thinking back over everything that's happened since Slade got out of the hospital. It's crazy how much has changed in such a short time.

Slade put in for a transfer from Indianapolis to Washington. It was approved, and we were lucky enough that his new office is only a forty-minute drive from our current town. We decided to look for a house that was at the halfway point between his office and the diner. We found the perfect one and closed on it a week ago. We waited until today to move because of the trial.

"Looks like you've been busy."

I whirl around at the sound of Slade's voice, and butterflies attack me from the inside out. "Little bit. Took a quick break to talk to Katelyn though."

"How're they doing with the baby?"

"Great. She's tired, but she's happy and that's all the matters."

"Are you happy?" Slade asks as he stalks toward me and runs his fingers up my sides.

My body immediately responds, and a shiver races up my spine. "So damn happy." My tone is breathy, giving away what he's doing to me.

"Me too."

Slade's mouth captures mine, and his tongue slides past my lips. The kiss seems to go on forever, and I'm certain that I'm going to be pinned against a wall quickly, but Slade pulls away, surprising me.

"If we keep going, we're never going to get out of here," he says with regret in his voice.

"And…" I taunt.

"And we've only got the truck for a few hours, so we better get moving."

I groan and pout, but the truth is, I'm ready to leave this apartment behind. There are some great memories here, but there are also some not so great ones. This new house is the fresh start we both need after everything.

"Lead the way."

Slade

When I pull the truck into the driveway of our new house, Brandie behind me in her SUV, my nerves kick into overdrive. I watch in the side mirror as she steps out of the vehicle and gazes at the house with a big smile on her face.

As she walks toward the truck, I get out, and together we walk to the front door. This is either going to be the best day of my life or the worst. After Detective Lee was sentenced to life in prison yesterday, I knew the timing was perfect. Who am I kidding? The time would have been perfect no matter what, but having that loose end tied up makes it even better.

"Are you ready?" I ask.

Brandie nods and I reach in my pocket for the key. My palms are sweaty, and the key slips from my grip and hits the ground. I bend to pick it up, the entire time trying to even out my breathing and chastising myself for letting my nerves get the best of me.

"Is everything okay?" she asks with genuine concern.

"Of course." *Other than my insides are in knots, and I feel like I'm going to throw up.*

"Okay."

I fit the key in the lock and turn the knob. I take a deep breath and hold it before shoving the door open and stepping aside for Brandie to go in ahead of me.

When she steps over the threshold, I hear her sharp intake of breath and release my own. I close the distance between us and settle my hands on her shoulders.

"When did you do this?" she asks.

I look beyond her into the living room and see the rose petals I spread in a path before I went to the apartment. They lead to the hallway where the master bedroom is. Brandie follows the trail, and when she reaches the bedroom door, she sees the envelope that's balanced between the knob and the door itself.

"What is this?" she asks over her shoulder.

"Open it and find out."

She tentatively reaches for the envelope and pulls her hand back as if it's going to burn her. After several false starts, she's got the paper in her hands and she's gingerly opening the flap.

"Brandie," she reads aloud. "We didn't meet under the best of circumstances, but that's okay. We met and that's all that matters. Before you, I was jaded and convinced that I was destined to grow old alone. But even with both of us having baggage from hell, we found something in each other that only we could recognize. We found love, and I will do anything and everything to make sure neither of us has to know what it's like to live without the other. I love you. Slade."

Brandie turns to me and there are tears in her eyes. "I love you, too," she chokes out.

"I know." I kiss her forehead. "But there's more."

Her eyes widen, and I instruct her to open the bedroom door. She slowly turns around and opens the set of french doors that lead to the master suite. Again, she gasps, and I know I did this right.

The room is bathed in candlelight, and shadows dance on the walls creating the perfect setting. Brandie walks to the bed, stopping just next to it. The bed is brand new, custom built for us, and on the mattress are the words 'Will you marry me' in even more rose petals.

She stares at the bed for a few moments, which gives me the opportunity to pull the ring out of my pocket and drop to one knee.

"Brandie?"

She turns around, and her hands fly to her mouth when she sees me.

"I meant what I wrote. I don't want to live a day in this life without you by my side. Will you marry me?"

Brandie drops to her knees and throws her arms around my neck.

"Yes. Of course, I'll marry you."

BONUS CHAPTER

Need more of Slade and Brandie? Sign up for my newsletter at andirhodes.com for an EXCLUSIVE bonus chapter, as well as updates on upcoming novels and giveaways.

SNEAK PEEK AT JETT'S GUARD

BOOK THREE IN THE BASTARDS AND BADGES SERIES

Jett...

Being a DEA agent is all I ever wanted. Undercover work was an added bonus that gave me the excuse needed to do whatever was necessary to take down the bad guys. But when a riot breaks out in the prison I'm at, I'm torn between my mission and the pretty guard who gets caught in the crossfire.

I never dreamed that, a year later, I'd end up living next door to her, let alone helping her work through her demons. All the while trying to chase away mine. The last thing I need is a woman in my life. Two years undercover has hardened me and stripped away at my soul. But here I am, tossed into the deep end and praying we can keep each other afloat.

Emma...

All I ever wanted to be when I grew up was an officer of the law. Prison guard was the job I got and I loved everything about it. That is, until the day my world shifted and I was thrown into chaos. The last person I expected to save me was the inmate I never could quite get a read on.

Trauma has a way of bringing life to a screeching halt. I shut the world out and locked myself in. That is, until I got a new neighbor. He pulled me from the darkness and I was drawn to him like a moth to a flame. Just when I think I'm safe and he's chased away my demons, I'm thrown back into hell with no idea how to get out. Will I be able to let him save me for a second time?

PROLOGUE

JETT

"Are you sure about this?"

I study Jackon and Slade for a moment before returning my attention to Special Agent in Charge, Timothy Bing. Based on the scowls on their faces, they aren't happy about needing help, but it would be impossible for them to do the job without being recognized.

"I'm sure." I flip through the pages of the file in front of me. "This guy was a cop?"

"A detective," Slade sneers.

"Damn," I mutter.

According to the file, Jeffrey Lee is currently serving a life sentence in a federal prison for human trafficking, kidnapping, attempted murder and fraud, among other things. He's also the biological son of Saul Luciano, a man that I, along with Jackson and Slade, put away last year. None of us knew about Jeffrey at the time, which makes sense considering he was given up for adoption at birth.

"How long will I be undercover?"

"As long as it takes," SAC Bing reports. "Obviously, this isn't the type of thing we'd normally get involved in as Lee's crimes aren't drug related, but, other than these two," he nods to indicate Jackson and Slade. "You have the most knowledge about the family and their operations. And Lee has never seen you, so it'll be easier for you to get what we need."

"And what exactly is it that we need?"

"We now know that Lee, alongside Sapphire and her father, had started to expand their *enterprise* across the country. We need you to get close to Lee and get him to open up to you, tell you who else is involved and locations of where they're housing the women."

"This guy was a detective. What makes you think he won't smell an undercover agent from a mile away? Clearly he knows how to blend in. I assume that also means he's more astute than this operation gives him credit for."

"Six months ago, that may have been the case, but he suffered massive injuries during the explosion that killed Sapphire, his biological sister. During interrogations, his memories seem to remain intact, but he's not firing on all cylinders."

"That doesn't necessarily make me feel better. If anything, that may make him more dangerous."

"Listen, Jett, if we didn't think you could handle it, we wouldn't have requested you," Jackson says. "I worked alongside you for a year, and I never had a clue that you were DEA. And I'm a damn good agent. If you fooled me, you can fool Jeffrey Lee."

I lean back in my chair and interlock my fingers behind my head. Lee seems to be a chip off the old block despite being adopted and raised by two loving parents who had nothing to do with the criminal underworld of his biological family. While he personally isn't going to be hurting anyone from a jail cell, that doesn't mean there aren't others on the outside that will on his and the Luciano family's behalf.

Images of the concrete rooms that housed the victims of this particular family flash through my mind. Katelyn and Brandie, the fiance's of Jackson and Slade respectively, were among the women taken and tortured by the Luciano's. The conditions were beyond disgusting, and each was degraded and treated like lesser beings than cockroaches. My stomach rolls at the thought of what they went through.

"What's my backstory?" I ask, leaning forward and resting my forearms on my knees.

SAC Bing slide's another file across the table. "It's all in there. We kept as much of your actual personal history as we could the same, to make it easier on you. You're in prison following a drug raid."

I skim through the words on the pages, and blood whooshes through my ears. I get tunnel vision as the details of my life before the DEA haunt me. I've always known, on some level, that the specifics weren't a secret, but to have it confirmed and used as part of an operation is unsettling.

"Will I have a contact in the prison?" I ask SAC Bing after slamming the file closed. I make a point of not looking at Jackson and Slade, unable to handle whatever pity I know will be on their faces.

"No. With Lee being former law enforcement, we don't want to take the chance that he's already got someone on the inside. No one there will know your true identity. I'll be your only point of contact. I'll visit you once a week, as your attorney, and you can call me when you're permitted phone calls."

"Jett, listen," Slade straightens in his chair. "I'd give anything to go in your place. Lee is bad news, and this isn't going to be easy. I'm not saying you can't handle it. It's just…" He scrubs his hands over his face in frustration.

"I think what he's trying to say is that this is going to be a lot different from our time undercover at The White Lily," Jackson explains. "We still had our freedom then. In prison, not only are you completely stuck, but you're also going to be in close proximity to some of the worst criminals there are. Your safety will be at risk every single day, and nine times out of ten, the threats to you won't be because of this case."

I shove up from my chair and start to pace the office. "Got it. It's going to be dangerous. I'm not some newbie agent that isn't fully aware of the risks." I pick up my cover story file. "In case you missed it, nothing in my life has been easy. I don't do *easy*." I tuck the folder under my arm and stride to the door. With my fingers wrapped around the knob, I glance over my shoulder. "When do I leave?"

"You'll be traveling to Washington state with Slade when he returns home. He'll handle getting things set up so you're on the first available transport from the local jail to the federal prison."

"Brandie and I have a flight back tonight. I already have your ticket. We'll pick you up at four-thirty, on our way to the airport."

"Then if you'll excuse me, I've got some things to take care of."

I yank open the door and make my way out of the building. I don't grab anything from my office because I won't need any of that where I'm going.

I review the operation in my head, over and over, while I make the necessary phone calls to make sure my rental home is packed up and belongings put in storage while I'm gone. I know from my time undercover before that SAC Bing will make sure that everything is handled properly and there are no loose ends.

Over the next forty-eight hours, I debate on calling my parents, letting them know I'm going to be out of touch for a while. I don't make the call though. They haven't given a shit about me in a long time. Hell, they hadn't even noticed that I'd been out of touch the last time.

When I step onto the bus transport, my hands and legs shackled, I shift my thoughts from my past to the task at hand. I've spent a lot of time in prisons, but never as a criminal. I'm not worried about being able to handle myself or keep any actual threats to my safety at bay.

I take in the few other prisoners around me. One guy looks like he's jonesing for his next fix, and another looks like he could use a hug from him mommy. A third guy is staring straight ahead, giving no indication that he's even aware that there are people around him. And the fourth guy looks like he could be my grandfather. If this is a representation of what lies ahead for me, I'll be just fine.

The bus slows to a stop, and a look out the window tells me we've arrived. For as far as I can see, there's barbed wire fencing atop what appear to be roughly twenty-foot-tall concrete walls. When we pass through the gates, I get my first glimpse of my new home. It's a goddamn fortress.

"We're here," the guard at the front of the bus says as he stands up. "Get your asses up and moving. We don't got all day."

I slowly walk down the center aisle of the transport. I'm the last prisoner to exit, and when I do, I'm immediately struck with a sense of dread. There are inmates lined up against the fence, catcalling and shouting at us. Some are sticking their tongues through the chain link fence and wiggling them in a suggestive manner.

The four others from the bus are definitely *not* an accurate representation.

When it's my turn to walk through the metal detectors to enter the prison, I hesitate for a moment. I'm shoved forward with something hard against my back and stumble when the chain between my ankles reaches its limit.

When I gain my balance, I notice the guard behind me holding a nightstick. His name tag identifies him as Officer Cox and the shit-eating grin on his face tells me he's someone I need to watch my back with.

He leans toward me and is inches from my face when he says, "Welcome to hell, inmate."

ABOUT THE AUTHOR

Andi Rhodes is an author whose passion is creating romance from chaos in all her books! She writes MC (motorcycle club) romance with a generous helping of suspense and doesn't shy away from the more difficult topics. Her books can be triggering for some so consider yourself warned. Andi also ensures each book ends with the couple getting their HEA! Most importantly, Andi is living her real life HEA with her husband and their boxers.

For access to release info, updates, and exclusive content, be sure to sign up for Andi's newsletter at andirhodes.com.

ALSO BY ANDI RHODES

Broken Rebel Brotherhood

Broken Souls

Broken Innocence

Broken Boundaries

Broken Rebel Brotherhood: Complete Series Box set

Broken Rebel Brotherhood: Next Generation

Broken Hearts

Broken Wings

Broken Mind

Bastards and Badges

Stark Revenge

Slade's Fall

Jett's Guard

Soulless Kings MC

Fender

Joker

Piston

Greaser

Riker

Trainwreck

Squirrel

Gibson

Satan's Legacy MC

Snow's Angel

Toga's Demons

Magic's Torment